**What **

All characters in this book are fictitious. Any resemblance to actual persons living or dead is coincidental.

Acknowledgments: Several of these stories have previously appeared in *Her Mother's Ashes*, Nur Jehan Aziz, editor (Toronto: TSAR Books, 1998), *Living in America*, R.R. Kerns, editor (Boulder CO: Westview Press, 1995), and *Toronto South Asian Review*.

Cover art: Christine Lynn, untitled ink and watercolour © 1998, CARCC. From the collection of Joe Blades.
Author photo by Peter Tittenberger, University of Winnipeg
Design and in-house editing by the publisher, Joe Blades
Proofreading by Julia Cool
Printed and bound in Canada by Sentinel Printing, Yarmouth NS

First printing 1999
This edition printed May 2001
This title is also published as Broken Jaw Press eBook 20 (ISBN 1-896647-56-1, PDF) with distribution via http://PublishingOnline.Com

The publisher gratefully acknowledges support from The Canada Council for the Arts and New Brunswick's Arts Development Branch.

Broken Jaw Press
Box 596 Stn A
Fredericton NB E3B 5A6
Canada
www.brokenjaw.com
jblades@nbnet.nb.ca
tel / fax 506 454-5127

Canadian Cataloguing in Publication Data
Uma Parameswaran.

What was always hers

(New muse award ; 1999)

ISBN 1-896647-12-X

PS8581.A688W5 1999　　C813'.54 C99-950222-0
PR9199.3.P367W5 1999

What Was Always HERS

Uma Parameswaran

Fredericton • Canada

For
Kausalya, Sivarajanna and Vasanti
storytellers par excellence

Contents

What Was Always Hers

Veeru heard the click of the light switch in the hallway. Niranjan quietly opened the door and came to bed in the dark. He sat on his side of the bed. Veeru waited for him to speak. Sitting on the bed instead of getting in was a cue, a preamble to a serious statement. Veeru turned just enough to let him know she was awake. She always was when he came to bed, though she had learnt to stay very still if she was disinclincd for any intimacy. As she had been the last six months.

She waited. She even moved to face him and said, "Hnh?" He sat on, silent. Then he got in, stroked her hair and turned his back to her. Veeru lay very still and wondered what he wanted to tell her. This was the third night in a row that he had sat on the bed and not spoken. A vague chill of the last time ran over her body. It was six months ago but each time it hit upon her consciousness it was like a fresh wound. "I think it is best that you end it," he had said, "I'll phone your doctor tomorrow. You know it is best done early in the first trimester."

She had given him the news the previous day, at his study table, with a catch of excitement. "Maybe, god willing, it will be a girl this time." He had shaken his head, without so much as a moment's pause. "Two are enough. We have two little nuggets of gold, why do we need another? *Hum doh, hamare doh*," he repeated the catchphrase that the government propaganda machine had plastered on every wall, every autorickshaw and bus in his student days — 'We two, ours two.' She tried to joke, "Oh, that is outdated. The current slogan is 'We are one, ours one.' And we've already broken the rule." Her eyes were filling with tears. He was more gentle now. "I too would have dearly loved it if one of the two had been a girl. But the fact is that we have two healthy, beautiful children, and that is enough. You wouldn't want to tempt fate, now would you?" He was targeting her deep-seated fears. And he hit home. Instinctively, her village-nurtured mind conjured up pictures of the two boys dead or dying, and she said, “Please god, grant me contentment with the gifts you have showered on us.”

Now, as she lay still, she thought, Oh, that was so manipulative of him. Curse him, curse him for the way he plays me like a fiddle.

She had brooded all night and every night since then. During the day, the routine helped her block out the baby, the physical pain that had healed, the other pain that would never heal. But at night, as she lay listening to the rustle of paper, the sound of his fingers on the computer, thoughts came again, the same sequence over and over again, night after night these six months. They lived here, here in Vancouver, British Columbia. One, two, three, it had no relevance. They could feed ten as easily as one. Free schooling, free medicare, free everything. This was the golden land of golden todays and tomorrows. Her mind had already raced to a bigger house the moment her doctor had confirmed her pregnancy. In Burnaby perhaps, or Coquitlam, marble staircase and four bedrooms, like Raminder’s, the gold streaked marbled tiles gleaming in the bathrooms. They could afford it, they could afford anything in this golden land where sea and mountain endlessly kissed each other in abandon.

Her village home was eight years behind her. She had grown immeasurably in those years. Thanks to him, one part of her mind said. He had persuaded, lyricised, nagged, praised, pushed her into growing, and she had. Thanks to him. Thanks to him, how many times had she told others that, and herself, and had meant it too. He was more than she could ever have imagined in a man, growing up in her little village on the Yamuna. Thanks to him, thanks to him.

But that wasn’t quite true. Within a week of her first visit, she had made a pact with the goddess, that she would make herself his real helpmeet, his equal so that he could achieve his fullest potential, for she knew that he was made for greatness. It was a surge of power she had felt as she made that promise. She did not swear that she would serve him and wait on him hand and foot, as any other woman in the village would have done. One week in this beautiful land — where sea and mountains and sky showered perennial benediction — one week in that student apartment — every surface strewn with newspapers or magazines or handbills printed for distribution among the farm labourers, with an endless stream of visitors debating, writing, quoting Ghalib and Shakespeare and Marx — and she knew she had to grow so she could walk hand in hand with this giant mind who was her husband.

And she has grown, she thought now, listening to Niranjan's even breathing.

She had gone back to India. Spent two days with her in-laws in Delhi on landing, as a dutiful daughter-in-law should, though it was two days too many away from her son. Vikram was then two and a half years old. Every day she had spent in Canada, her heart had cried at their separation. She spent six weeks with her parents. Then she had gone again to Delhi with Vikram, for a short visit, she thought, so Vikram could be with his other grandparents for some time.

She learnt a great many things about the family, and each detail made her realize how lucky she was to have entered their family which was now hers.

Niranjan's parents lived in Safdarjang Enclave. They had built their house when the area had just been developed, when land was cheap and construction costs reasonable. It was a sprawling house, like those around, built for the future, when each of the four sons would have his own family suite of rooms. Like all the houses around, it had a smaller house at the back: first the small two room house was meant for servants, but as years went by and the cost of living and of rents skyrocketed, this structure was built into a flat, then the upstairs was built up and then a third floor, with a barsaati on the terrace, as with most houses on the street, and the rents helped pay for the escalating prices of basic commodities.

Niranjan's people were city people, had been for three generations. All his brothers and brothers-in-law were in business of one kind or another, two brothers managing the family business of electrical appliances. Niranjan was the black sheep of the family: he wanted to be a college professor; fortunately, he was the third son, and since the older two were already excited about the family business, Niranjan's impractical ideals could be indulged in. Everyone indulged Niranjan: he was that kind of person, intense, argumentative, and totally inept when it came to the pragmatic realities of life. Sisters and sisters-in-law always made sure he had hot meals even if he came home, as he often did, long after the servant had left for the evening.

When it was time for Niranjan to get married, there was no dearth of options. Girls whose parents had a family background similar to theirs, who had houses as big as theirs in Greater Kailash I or II, girls who were studying at Lady Shri Ram or Miranda House, and looked as beautiful as the ceramic figurines that Niranjan's father had brought from England back in the 1950s. Girls who spoke English with a good Convent accent, girls who knew how to cook and sew, studying as they were towards a Home Science degree, recently renamed Home Economics.

But Niranjan would have none of them. He was dedicated to village-uplift work, and he thought their native village was the most beautiful place for anyone to grow up in. His father had sold his land years ago, to build the house in Delhi, but there was still an uncle who lived on ancestral land. The old man had come up with the name of his best friend, whose grand daughter, Veeru, was exactly what Niranjan would want in a wife — she was bright, she was intelligent, and she was lucky. And he went on to list all the various and varied fortunes she had brought to her family over the years. "The day she was born was the day the monsoons came at last, after a drought that seemed it would never end. The day of her naming ceremony, the jewel on the crown of the village deity that had disappeared four years earlier, had magically reappeared on the crown, loosely placed in the delicate gold claws from which it had been wrested. When she had just started to crawl, she had toddled off to alert others that grandpa had fallen off his chair: he had had a stroke and thanks to the baby he could be helped rightaway, and he lived another twelve years. Our child Veeru will bring good fortune to any man who clasps her hand in marriage. Believe you me," he said, "our child Veeru will make a palace of any house she enters."

Niranjan's sisters and sisters-in-law smiled and snickered into their dupattas as Uncle went on and on, because they knew Niranjan's parents would leave the choice entirely to Niranjan and that he would laugh at the superstitious drivel and marry one of the chic young women from Miranda House. But he didn't.

He went to the village and met Veeru. True, the meeting was more a meeting with her parents the first time, but he went again and then once more, and managed to talk to her. He even managed to get them to send her to Delhi for a visit to her aunt who lived not too far from them. He then took her to Talkatora Gardens one Saturday afternoon, to tell her about his plans, of which he had many and all very neatly tied and labelled — he would go abroad to study, come back with a PhD, get a job in one of the colleges in Delhi, and then would be home free, to continue his village-uplift programs. That meant he could not guarantee anyone anything, except his undying devotion to any woman he married and any children they might have. He had already taken a vow of service to the community, and nobody could change that. "Like Vinobaji," she said. That sealed his answer. He would marry Veeru and no one else. Any girl of seventeen who in the year 1978 knew about Vinobaji was a gem too precious to ignore. And so they were married.

And she brought him luck. When he returned to Delhi after the wedding, he found a letter waiting — the University of British Columbia had not only accepted him for graduate study but had said it would give him an assistantship. Coming as it did after rejections from a dozen other universities in the United States during the year before he met Veeru, even Niranjan was inclined to believe a little of what Uncle had bragged about Veeru being a lucky person. It took him six months to get all his documents, and then he was gone, and Veeru went back to her parents' house. He returned for a four week holiday a year later, and Veeru joined him in Delhi, and she conceived. When Vikram was born, back in the village, Niranjan's parents, who never travelled except for a family wedding, drove down from Delhi, and there was a week-long celebration.

When Vikram was two, Niranjan arranged for Veeru to visit him. She stayed with him for four memorable months. Everything was new, everything was wonderful, and she loved every minute of every day.

Jitin and Demmi were the first people that Veeru met when Niranjan brought her to his apartment from the airport. It was a Thursday. While Niranjan went down to get the suitcases, the two young women welcomed her. Veeru was pleased to see brown faces. Oh how she wished she could tell her new friends all about her airplane journey and the sea of white faces and the stewardesses with their incredibly impeccable uniforms and solicitous smiles, and the way the earth stretched under them and how the cities at night were like a star-studded sky each time they landed. But she kept quiet, thinking they would laugh at her.

"I am sure you would like a cup of tea," Demmi said, without making a move from her chair. Demmi was amply endowed on all fronts, and overflowed the seat of the chair.

Veeru looked around the kitchen and said to Jitin, "Deedi, I am so glad you are here to teach me everything."

Demmi laughed. When she smiled, there were two deep dimples that formed, despite her chubby cheeks.

Jitin went to the stove, on which they had already got the dinner ready, and put on a saucepan of water. "The first and perhaps the only thing you need to learn rightaway is to make tea," Demmi said. "You'll need to make gallons and gallons of tea on Saturday and every weekend for the rest of your stay here." Veeru stood next to Jitin, watching her, as she placed an electric kettle of water on the counter and plugged it in. "This is for Niranjan, who likes angrezi tea but the rest of us like our masala tea." Jitin increased the flame. "This is just like our Burshane back home," Veeru said shyly. "Yes, exactly. The only difference is that there is always a pilot flame burning," she pointed to the pilot flame, "and before leaving the house or going to bed, you must make sure it is not out. And here is the oven pilot," she added, opening the oven door and showing Veeru. "Very, very important that you get into the habit of checking the oven pilot," Demmi said. "And don't stick your head into the oven, unless you want to do yourself in," Jitin added. Demmi tsk, tsked. "What kind of talk is that, to a new bride and all?" Jitin shrugged. "I have often thought about it. The best way to go, painless, like falling asleep and not waking up."

Veeru answered Demmi, having lost Jitin. "Not new, you know, little Vikram will soon be three." Even as she said it, her voice choked, remembering her baby.

Niranjan came in, carrying her suitcases, just a little out of breath. He looked around, growled like a tiger and said, "Now who has been making my young bride cry?" Veeru smiled and said, "It is just stupid me, thinking of little Vikram." Niranjan took a sip of water, went to the telephone and dialled his parents. He told them Veeru had arrived safely etc. and would they please write to Veeru's parents rightaway. At which, Veeru cried again.

Demmi and Jitin set the table for dinner, and wanted to leave but Niranjan insisted they stay for dinner. "I'll just have a quick shower," he said.

Veeru lay on the bed, thinking she would rest till he came out, but her eyes closed and would not open. She heard them laugh at how tired she was, poor thing, and heard their voices for a few moments before falling into a drugged jet-lag sleep.

Niranjan lived in an apartment that was the first floor of a small house. Most other Indian students lived closer to the university, in apartment blocks all of which were identical with their closed-in hallways and faintly musty carpets smelling of foods from many lands. But Niranjan's place was an old house that looked as though it should be boarded up lest part of it fall on people's heads as they walked up the sidewalk from the driveway to the front door; but it was airy inside, with windows on all four sides, albeit with motheaten woodwork. The landlady lived downstairs; though she was a cheerful capable woman as handy with tools as any man, she was just too short of cash to put in new windows or indulge in any kind of major repair. She had four children and eight or nine grandchildren in different parts of the province and was often away, visiting them.

Niranjan's apartment was a hive of activity, with people dropping in all times of the day. Soon it was clear to Veeru why Niranjan had not completed his studies and come home as he had planned the summer Vikram was conceived. He had taken to labour activism and his thesis work had been put on the back burner. For the first month or two, Veeru did not know much about what his activist work involved.

She was told on the very first day that they were organizing a huge rally three weeks from thence. There was a lot to be done, as evident from the number of cardboard cartons that were transported from and into the house. Handbills were handwritten in Punjabi and run off in hundreds of copies. The people who came to the apartment were a wide medley but everyone seemed totally dedicated to the work and thought Niranjan a leader. Veeru had never seen white people in India, nor Chinese or Japanese, nor indeed even Indians from the deep south or Bengal. It was like going to the village fair every day, except that the fair came to them. There were eight women among the twenty or so in Niranjan's work group. They took Veeru in hand, teaching her the ins and outs of cooking in a Canadian kitchen, in a student kitchen, they added. And when Veeru visited other Indian houses, she knew what they meant. The other houses were big, with two car garages and two kitchens, two dining tables, two of everything including sinks in the kitchen and bathroom, or so it seemed to Veeru. But she would not have traded Niranjan's little hole for anything in the world. The working group people were warm, hard-working, and their tongues worked as hard as their hands as they folded and stacked the handbills and mounted charts and maps on photograph easels which they transported around for their weekend work in the farms and lumber belt. Most of the workers were Indians, and she felt she was back in the village, except that young men in the village would never have come into her mother's kitchen and talked so freely and loudly.

Two of the eight women were older. For Veeru, they made a special effort and mixed a bit of Hindi in their Punjabi. Three others were young and white. Two of them spoke to her very slowly, with a lot of sign language and laughs, to get her to understand English. So did the white men, and them she did not even hear for the first month, so overcome was she with shyness at her ignorance, and awe at their huge white bodies. But the third white girl, Lisa, spoke to her as she spoke to anyone else, and for that Veeru loved her, and felt she understood her better than anyone else, not the words, which flew over her head, but the meaning.

The woman to whom Veeru took rightaway was Jitin. Jitin was a natural leader; she not only ordered people about in the living room but she managed much of the kitchen work, for of course there was an endless stream of snacks and tea all day during the weekends. Jitin was the kitchen master and assigned jobs as and when necessary. She was a no-nonsense kind of person most of the time, her hair combed back from her large flat forehead and tied back in a tight pony tail. Feature by feature, she was not good looking. Her nose was rather too long, her forehead rather too flat, her body rather angular even though she had full, firm breasts. But she had a charisma that made her beautiful in Veeru's eyes, the personality of one who was in control of herself, her surroundings, a leader. She wore blue denim jeans and an Indian top, the kind that were piled high in the little stores along Janpath, delicate prints on thin cotton, with a smock collar neck. Often she wore thick denim shirts, with just a wisp of a flower to show it was a girl's shirt and not a man's. She was so obviously in charge and respected by the others that Veeru gravitated towards her for the answers to all her questions. Veeru loved to watch Jitin and she wished Jitin would laugh more often; the laugh that drove away the sadness from that lovely face; it was not the sound, which was short and suppressed, but the way it lighted her face, blotted out that unfathomable sadness that dwelt in her eyes those times she seemed to withdraw into her private unfathomable world.

That first weekend, when Veeru called her Jitin Deedi, Jitin laughed. Just call me Jitin, she said. But Deedi, you are so much wiser than I am, Veeru said shyly. Jitin looked away, staring out the window. And now she was not a no-nonsense person but someone else; she had a faraway sad look, the brown flecks of her eyes took on a dark hue as though the sun had set. Then she turned and laughed and the kitchen light brought back the brown flecks, and she said, "But in this country everyone calls everyone else by just their first name."

Despite which Veeru got a title that stuck. Rahim, a very young man with long curly hair and a stubble, was all over her like a little puppy that had found a friend. That first weekend, even before Veeru had got over her jet lag, the working group came in the morning and stayed all day. After the introductions, while Niranjan, who was called Boss by everyone, was going over the day's agenda, Rahim slipped away and came back with a posie of flowers stolen from a neighbour's garden. "For you, bibiji," he said with a flourish and everyone clapped.

Veeru was amused. Only Niranjan's mother was given that title, and now here she was, Bibiji. She laughed, and the others laughed with her, equally amused at the grandiose title for this wisp of a girl who still looked the same as the small little peasant in the wedding photographs that Boss had brought back four years ago.

"Bibiji this, bibiji that," Rahim hovered around her, showing her sleight of hand card tricks, running out to buy some "absolutely out-of-this-world ice cream" that Bibiji had to taste that very minute ... The name stuck. Bibiji. The men, young and old, called her that.

*****

Those four months in Vancouver provided Veeru with enough fodder to regale her village aunts and friends for a whole month. Our Veeru bitiya, they said, our own little bitiya had not only crossed the seas to see the world but has come back pregnant. Smart little one.

Veeru had landed in Delhi and had spent only two days there, eager to get back to her son. Back in the village, she relaxed into the old routine. For some reason, this time she was even more plagued by morning sickness that the first time. This foreign baby, they teased her, was already choosy and finicky, they said, not letting their Veeru bitiya eat mangoes or chutney or drink sweet lassi. But once she got over the third month, she felt she should go to Delhi, take Vikram to his other grandparents for a short visit, so she thought.

After two weeks in Delhi, the village seemed far too stifling; Veeru remembered her pact with the goddess and her ambitions got re-ignited. She decided she needed to stay in Delhi. She started being extra attentive to her mother-in-law's needs, hovered around her, peeled the oranges just right, hurried ahead of her senior sister-in-law to make the carrot juice that both parents had in the morning before the servants came in, pressed her mother-in-law's feet, asked her to tell her stories from long ago so Vikram and she could know more about Niranjan. She wrote to her parents that her in-laws wanted her to stay longer, and she told her in-laws that her brothers were too busy to escort her back home. All of which was rather unnecessary because both parties believed she really belonged at her in-laws' and it was only Niranjan's decision that came in the way. He insisted she should stay with her parents, without any pressures of city life or in-laws.

Niranjan's parents were extremely nice people. When Veeru had gone back to the village after Niranjan's departure for the States, Veeru told her village aunts about the big house and about them, about how she was treated so well by Niranjan's sisters and sisters-in-law in spite of being the youngest daughter-in-law. They said, "Veeru bitiya, we always knew you were lucky. But don't go about bragging lest you tempt fate: keep all this good fortune to yourself." The more Veeru knew them, the more she appreciated their values, their culture, their love.

Now, when Veeru hinted that Vikram was really happy in Delhi, and maybe school here would be better than at the village, Niranjan's parents were delighted. Write to Niranjan, they said. While she struggled with herself as to how she should word the letter, the obstetrician who had birthed almost every baby in the Anand family for the last twenty years, was not at all pleased at the prospect that any Anand baby should be born in a village. Everyone was pleased as can be. Of course she should stay in the city. It was all settled. Niranjan's father took the decision and wrote to Niranjan. If as a new bride, she had been treated with indulgence, as the pregnant wife of an absent son, she was treated even more so. And Vikram, who was the spitting image of his father, as each one said at least once a day, was as loved and popular as Niranjan had been.

Veeru set about educating herself. She read just about everything she could lay her hands on in her in-laws' home. But all the nephews and nieces went to English medium schools and there weren't that many books in Hindi, though the circulating library man brought in new magazines every other day. If you live in Canada and want to be an activist you can't do diddly unless you learn to speak Punjabi, Niranjan had said, and so she got herself both an English teacher and a Punjabi master. Her parents-in-law were indulgent: they had always lived in the city, and they loved this poor sweet child from the village who was so eager to learn. They treated her more as a daughter than as a daughter in law, for Niranjan's sake.

Grow, grow, she had grown. So that, when she came again in 1985 to join Niranjan and set up her own household with husband and children, she came as she had promised the goddess she would — as a helpmate for her husband who was destined for greatness. Over the next few years, she became the group's most untiring worker; she organized and reorganized their papers, neatly filing everything. She typed up handbills, learnt to format the newsletter, found the cheapest, most reliable printing place. She went on to find out more about fundraising; more about possible speakers and strategies for rousing the farm labourers into protesting the use of pesticide; petitioning for better conditions for migrant fruit pickers; getting English classes started for families who had been in B.C. for three generations without ever bothering to learn the language ... Both her Punjabi and her English improved with time because she had to use both languages every day. She learnt to drive, and was behind the wheel every weekend, as Niranjan sat beside her poring over his notes and the boys sat at the back singing "Ten bottles of beer on the wall" or some such song till their throats were hoarse. They went all over the southern part of the province until "Veeru Deedi" became a household word in many an Indian cabin and home in the fruit belt.

Grow, grow. She had grown, she thought, to be what she was born to be. But no. When Niranjan sat on the edge of the bed and said he would arrange with the doctor, she had to start all over again. With those few words, he had unravelled the tapestry of seven years, no much more than that, and she had spontaneously said, "God grant me contentment ..." She was no better than the farm labourers who talked about God's will and contentment and fate and gratitude in order not to do anything to speak up for themselves. She had to start all over again, as though she was once again an eighteen-year-old newcomer in that sprawling house in Safdarjang Enclave with an intense husband who was packing up to leave for god knew how long. With those five words, he had unravelled the tapestry of twice five years.

Murderer. That is the word that hammered at her heart every time she thought of it. Murderer. But she had acquiesced in the act of murder. She had allowed them to tear her child out and throw her into the incinerator. Strange, how these people who gave dogs and cats a burial could have the heart to throw away a child as though it was not a child.

Murderer. She could not bear his presence. She brooded over all the incidents over the years when he had played her like a fiddle, made all the decisions for their common good as he always said, but her mind now grown to understanding, realized all decisions were always on his own.

First, because she was convalescing, and then for no overt reason, they stayed on their own sides of the bed after the abortion, and though Niranjan invariably stroked her hair or back before turning over, and she acknowledged it noncommittally, they seemed to have arrived at some mutual agreement.

Or so she thought for six months. Until the night he spoke.

"We have to end this," he said.

Something in Veeru sighed with relief. Yes, they had to end this stalemate: she had to stop thinking of him as a murderer. Life had to go on, though they had extinguished one life. They, she thought, she had at last arrived at the point when it was not "he" but they, together, had done what had been done. What could not, cannot be undone.

She stretched her hand from under the blanket and reached for his lap as he sat there, on his side of the bed. He raised her hand to his cheek, and then let it drop on his lap. She could feel the lint specks on his flannel pyjamas.

"We must file for divorce," he said, "and it is best we do it soon and get it over with."

Veeru lay very still; she should withdraw her hand, she thought, but it lay heavy on his lap, numb, even though she could still feel the lint specks.

"It is long overdue, Veeru; I cannot go on, torn between the two of you."

Veeru trembled. Two? what did he mean, two? Jitin, of course Jitin. Who else could it be?

He continued, slowly, haltingly, even though he had probably rehearsed the words every night for who knows how long. He paused at times, as though waiting for her to say something, anything, but she kept quiet and still. Oh the power of silence when the other wanted a response, any response but silence. "From the very first day I met her, we both knew, and because we knew we dared not spend any time together, and because we knew, we couldn't talk about it. It isn't as though we didn't try to break it off, we tried the best we could. That is why I had you come over that summer, to break the endless cycle of frustration, of trying to break off and not being able to, and not being able to talk about it though each knew there could be no other. (No other? no other? what was I then? sleeping with you every night for four months) And then after you left ..." he paused. (Oh my god, that was seven years ago, for seven years ...)

"Six years is a long time," he said. "And it isn't fair to her (to her, she thought, to her, what am I?) We are not getting any younger, and she has a right to her child, and to all that has always been hers ..." (What is he saying? she is expecting, oh my god, she is carrying his child.)

A vicious anger tore at her vitals. Murderer, murderer. How dare you let her child live after killing mine.

"She wants to get married, and I have to be fair, we have waited so long." (Why need you go through such a sham? and who cares if one is married or not, this is Canada.)

"I don't know why I thought I could eat my cake and have it too," he said lamely. "That we could go on as we've been, but she will not have it that way. How can I be a hypocrite, she says, preach one thing and practise another, and she is right. Not just a teacher but a counsellor too, at an inner city school."

He paused. "There never is a right time for this. Every time I wanted to tell you, something or other came up — my mother's illness, your father's death, your long visit to India, Vikram spraining his ankle at the rink ... (my abortion, say it, say it, abortion of my beautiful baby at your hands) and all the commitments we have big and small, every weekend ... So I ask you, Veeru, I ask you please to let me go."

No, she thought with a wild strangled scream of hatred that she alone could hear. No, I won't let you go. Let her child be a bastard, as though that has any meaning here in Canada, but yes, since it does mean something to her and to you, go stew your hearts out. My answer is, No.

"I don't expect any answer right now," he said softly, sadly. "But please think about it, please."

He got into bed. Veeru clutched at her pillow. Six, seven, eight years, and she had not known. How could she not have known?

Please think about it, please, he'd said. How different from six months ago when he had merely stated that he would phone her doctor. How small he was, as he lay curled with his back to her, and how huge he had seemed that night six months ago. She felt herself grow, grow meaner and bigger and wilder. No. Never. Power. This was power at last. She would wield it. And the voice kept hissing, seven years, where had she been? Jitin, Jitin, the very first person she had met in this country, the person she had doted on as Deedi, deedi, even though Jitin had never allowed her to call her so. Perhaps because she knew how ironically right that was — older sister, who had already been with him. Not strictly true, she thought with a dull pang, remembering he had told her the actual relationship had started only after that summer. Liar, she thought, liar. But she knew he was not lying.

That wonderful summer, then, was nothing? She had been just a ploy, a pawn they had brought into play to try head off something, if they really wanted to head it off, that is. Liar. Except that she knew he wasn't.

Jitin. How often in those days she had run to her both literally and in thought, to sort out problems, little lessons in how to cope with a new land, a new everything. But now she remembered too how Jitin did not embrace her when greeting or taking leave the way the other women did. And yet, when she had been crying with homesickness and longing for her baby, and Jitin had figured it out just by her voice on the phone, she had come straight from school and Veeru had burst into tears all over again and Jitin had held her in her arms. That summer too, when Niranjan had been upset about something, Veeru had called up Jitin and Jitin had come over. "It scares me when he gets so intense about his work," she said, and Jitin had said, "I know what you mean. He can be rather intimidating, but you must trust him." And Veeru had calmed down then, but now thinking about it, she remembered Jitin's voice, the voice of one who knew someone's most intimate idiosyncrasies.

There must have been so many other times, Veeru thought. Yes, of course; at the beginning, she had been puzzled, upset at the way Niranjan turned to Jitin for everything, put his hand on her shoulder when consulting her. When she had hesitantly told one of the women about her fears, they had laughed it away. This is Canada, they said, and a man's hand on a woman's shoulder meant no more than on a man's. And Jitin, oh no, Jitin was hardly a woman, just look at her, all bones and brains, don't worry, she is just one of the boys. They themselves hugged and kissed Niranjan, with endearments — kanhaiya, Boss-baba, pyarelalla. And he was always warm and considerate to them, to everyone. And she had been reassured: they were older women, they wouldn't lie to her.

She had been meeting or phoning Jitin every single day for the first year or two. Jitin. Jitin. And even later, when they met less frequently, Jitin was the calm village pond to which she had retreated in moments of stress — with pink lotuses and wide green leaves, the clear cool water in which she took a dip before entering the village shrine. Jitin, Jitin. And now she had to hate her. Veeru lay very still all night, spewing hatred on Niranjan and Jitin by turns. At last it was morning and she entered into her safety net of routine. Breakfast for the children, laundry, vacuum, and thankfully it was her day to volunteer at the day-care.

Two weeks passed. Once again, Niranjan sat on the bed. "Have you thought about it?" he asked.

The answer is NO, she wanted to scream, I will not let you go. But she said nothing.

He spoke with long pauses.

"Nothing will change except that I won't be here at night. You can stay here; I think it is best not to disturb the boys' routine. Tell me what you would like me to do, what you need, and I will make sure you have it. The house, an allowance that will let you live in the same fashion as we are living now ... that is only fair. I don't need anything: I have my job and my needs are not much ... I will take care of anything that has to be done for the boys, for you, your travels, everything. If it is all right by you, I'd like to come often and spend time with the boys, but again, I will not insist. Anything you think is best for them is fine by me ..."

She did not reply. She merely turned over to show she was awake and then lay still.

Two months went by. She'd have started showing, Veeru thought, and went to places where she might run into Jitin. She saw her at the grocery store. But she looked as slim as ever. That weekend she went to the open air workshop that Niranjan was holding for fruit farm workers to protest the use of pesticides. Jitin was there, lifting easels on which they had mounted charts of statistics and photographs of victims. She was wearing a short top over her jeans, and every time she raised her hand to mount a graphic, there was a fleeting exposure of her waist above the jeans. Flat, flat as ever. Veeru left quietly, unable to bear the sight of the woman who seemed to have grown lovelier than ever before, and so far away, so so far away.

That night Niranjan came to the kitchen as she was cleaning up. "I thought I saw you at the workshop," he said.

"Yes," she said. Oh the power of silence when someone wanted you to speak.

And then the desire to taunt overcame her. "You shouldn't let her do so much heavy work," she said, "in her delicate condition."

"She's getting over it," he said, "it was a bad attack of stomach flu, but she's getting over it. Did you talk to her then?"

Veeru kept quiet. Was she not pregnant? Hadn't he said she was? Just a false alarm, was it? And was that why he hadn't been nagging her to give an answer? "No, I didn't. I didn't stay at all." Was she apologizing as though she ought to have spoken to her?

Niranjan stood for a while and then left.

Had he not said she was pregnant? Had he? Of course he had. She has a right to her child as indeed to all that has always been hers. Which didn't at all mean she was but only that she wanted to be.

Another week went by. It was surprising how they could continue to live in the same house, sleep in the same bed, as though he had not said what he had said that night three months ago. At breakfast and dinner, the boys spoke nonstop as they always did, and Niranjan joined them at their television shows and video games as he had always done. He took them to their hockey practice and swimming lessons, as always, and they came home laughing and singing as always.

Maybe they could continue to live this way. But Niranjan was getting impatient. "Give us our freedom," he said, every morning as he left for work. And every morning she wanted to scream on hearing those words. He did not say my freedom but our. Our freedom, he did not mean freedom for her and him but for Jitin and him. The sense of power that she had felt the first few days had palled. And now, it seemed Jitin was not expecting after all. Why couldn't he have let things be? Why did he have to tell her and telling erase away seven years of her life, no ten.

Veeru saw Jitin again that Friday. Veeru had been invited to join a committee on the working conditions of domestics. She did not know Jitin was a member. Would she have accepted the invitation had she known?

As she entered the room and joined others at the coffee table, she saw Jitin standing at the window; she looked tired, and forlorn, and utterly beautiful. She could not take her eyes off Jitin, but when Jitin was about to turn, Veeru turned away and spoke with the women next to her with more energy than the occasion warranted. Deedi, deedi, her heart cried out, and she longed to run to her. Several times during the meeting, she tried to concentrate on the cool efficient Jitin who was running the meeting but the image of the tired, lonely, utterly beautiful woman who had been standing at the window kept intruding, as did that yearning to embrace her. And she remembered another time. This was several years ago, maybe the second year of her arrival. For many days, she had not met Jitin; Jitin had not phoned her or responded to the messages Veeru had left on her answering machine. When they did meet, Veeru was solicitous. You don't look well, Jitin, she'd said, have you come down with something? the Asian flu that's been going around? And Jitin had tears in her eyes. Veeru had impulsively reached out to her, and for a moment Jitin had allowed her to hold her hands, and then had smiled and collected herself. "My little sister," she had said. And Veeru's heart had danced with joy.

Deedi, deedi. They were sisters. Could they not share one more thing? And be friends, sisters? No. Because they had shared it already, unbeknownst to Veeru. That was why they could not be friends. The hypocrisy of it all. But what could Jitin have done? Proposed a ménage á trois? And how would Veeru have responded? How else could she respond now other than the way she was? Had she been the village girl she was when she first landed here, would things have been different? Now, she had grown, grown out of her childhood view of life, her village views, how could she respond except with shock and revulsion and hate, hate for Jitin, for Niranjan, hate, hate. Even if she desired more intensely than ever before to regain what she had had with Jitin, even more intensely, it seemed than she longed for the Niranjan of old, that god who had taken her by the hand and raised her to his sky. More than for him, but that was because he was and always would be with her, because of the boys: whereas Jitin was gone, vanished like the rainbow that arced across the horizon of her childhood. Always pining for lost worlds, pining in those early years for her aunts' arms, for the placid dewlaps of Amrita, Devika, Latika ... cows she had named and fed and milked in those days which had vanished like the rainbows that arced across childhood horizons.

As she got into her Volvo after the meeting, inserted the key into the ignition and heard the purr of the engine as the car glided out, she felt power again, the power of how far she had come, how she had become the woman she was born to be, self-confident, energetic, a pro at the art of speaking, of sizing up her audience and speaking in their language: she had carefully crafted herself into her role by growing, growing to become the woman she was born to be. A jilted wife, she thought, was that what she was born to be? Rage, jealousy and hatred washed over her again.

But they could not wash away the ache of separation. Deedi, deedi. If she could just rest her head against Jitin's bosom and make time stand still. If she could just draw Jitin to her heart and make time stand still.

When she reached home, Vikram and Adarsh were at the dining table, with huge scoops of ice cream overflowing their bowls. "Oh, oh!" Vikram said, hearing her open the door from the garage. Adarsh waved his spoon. "We missed you, mom. Come, come this is scrumtious. Vik, bet you can't spell it." Vikram was into spelling competitions. He got off the hook by scoffing, "Sure can. *You* need to learn how to pronounce it right. Scrumptious."

Adarsh was at the counter, reaching out for a bowl for her. Ice cream was dripping down his milk moustache onto his pyjama top. "I love you," he said, smiling his new gap toothed smile. She kneeled and swept him into her arms, and gave him a bear hug, squeezing his body which still had baby fat. "Oh Addu, my baby, my sweetie, I love you too."

"I love you bigger than Canada."

"I love you bigger than India."

"I love you bigger than the moon."

"I love you bigger than the sun."

"I love you bigger than the stars."

"I love you bigger than the sky."

"I love you bigger than the UNIVERSE." They said the last line in unison.

It was an old ritual, from the days when her English had been a constantly garbled translation from Hindi. Vikram was too old for it now, but Adarsh had to say it at least once a day to each of his parents.

"Momma, can I sleep in the big bed today?" The bear hug had reminded him he had missed something of late. Weekends he would thromp, thromp into the big bed in the morning, and Vikram would sneak in too, scoffing but eager, and they would jump up and down on their father's back. The big bed. The other beds had their owner's names — Vikram's, Addu's, guest room, but the parents' was the big bed, as though it was common property. "Yes, yes," she said, "How about tomorrow morning?" She crushed him to herself, and always alert to Vikram's needs, she went over and hugged him. And she longed to feel Addu's cuddly body next to hers, and remembrances washed over her, Vikram's impatient mouth tugging at her breasts, the heaviness of full term, the ache in the small of the back, maid servants' expert hands massaging her feet, our Veeru bitiya has Goddess Lakshmi's magic touch of fortune, our bitiya ...

*****

Veeru was never clear why she agreed. Or maybe she didn't want to be clear about why. It was a bit of this and a bit of that. "If 'twere done when 'tis done, then 'twere well it were done quickly," Rahim used to say it for any number of things, from taking important decisions over which they'd argued the whole day to sealing envelopes with a thump.

The speed with which Niranjan acted once she agreed filled her once again with toxic hate, making her wish she could unsay what she had said, but she had agreed and faster than lightning, Niranjan had gone to India, come back and moved out. Later, she came to know that he had not told his parents the reason for his flying visit until his return.

*****

Veeru was in her cubicle at the office. She had just managed to shake Gerald off, just as she had to shake him off every morning. Gerald was a colleague, very handsome, very well-dressed, very competent, who had been top salesman of the month more often than anyone else in the two years that she had been there. Veeru wouldn't admit to herself that the reason she had become such a tasteful dresser, so careful about the quality and colours of her accessories and make-up was because as she stood in front of her clothes closet, she could imagine his eyes quickly taking her in each morning. He was always one of the first to be at the office, and she one of the last. He would come to her cubicle every morning within minutes of her arrival, as though by chance, but she knew he waited every morning for her, and if she did not come by nine-thirty, he would be at the front desk for some reason or another, waiting for her to appear, after which he would go away as though he had not been waiting for her.

Over the last few months, half in jest, half in earnest he had been courting her with his plan to start his own agency with her as his business and domestic partner. But Veeru had always been careful to flirt outrageously with him in the office so that everyone knew it was mere flirtation. She did not want to look at it seriously, even to herself, in case she found out that after Niranjan there could be no other that she could come close to or allow to come close to her. No, she did not want to be a martyr, one of those village women who crawled back to their husbands after being beaten black and blue, or who remained grass widows while the men consorted with devadasis. Just for that, she sometimes wished she would find someone, but not yet, and Gerald was not the one, not yet.

She replaced the receiver after talking to a client, and leaned back. The deal was going well. Mrs. Summers liked the house: Veeru had talked her into thinking it was okay to have a sauna just off the living room, where the present owner had put it because he was a partying person. One could talk a client into anything, Veeru thought happily, one kind of client that is.

She switched on the answering machine, having heard it beep during her conversation. It was Pritpal, one of the current group of workers around Niranjan. Veeru dialled the number she had been left. It was a downtown number.

"Veeru? is that Veeru?" Pritpal said twice, as though she had already forgotten her voice, Veeru thought with some bitterness.

"Yes," she replied, "yes, this is Veeru."

"I don't know how to tell you this," the voice hesitated, "Boss has been in an accident."

Veeru's heart missed a beat. Habit, one of the habits that remain long after they should, she thought, that reflexive throb of fear, so what if he has fallen off some ladder he was always climbing. Why call me? Call her, his wife, she wanted to say, but as always she said nothing, and waited though her heart thudded what when where how is he? She did not want idle gossip to spread about how rattled she had sounded asking what when where, as though she were still his wife.

"He is still in the hospital, but soon we'll be ... they'll be taking him," Pritpal broke down.

"To surgery? Is it that bad? Where?" Veeru tried to keep her voice efficient, and being at the office helped. Momma, you sound so different when you phone from your office, Adarsh had said just yesterday.

"Worse, much worse ..." Pritpal's voice trailed off into sobs, as the line clicked off.

*****

The phone was ringing when she entered the house. It was Niranjan's father. The line, full of static, crackled and waned as they sought to identify each other. "We got the news, Veeru," and then it was his mother. "Veeru *bahu*," she still called her that, "our hearts go out to you and the children, what can we say? I wish we could have seen him, that we could be there, I wish, oh my dear girl ..." And then his father again, "I am calling to find out details, nothing can be done, we know, and I don't want to impose on you, beti, but our old parent hearts need to know what happened. I have been calling every five minutes these last six hours from the moment we got the news, and you've been away."

Veeru sighed. "I don't know, Bappaji, I ... I heard it myself only a few minutes ago and I have just come home, I don't know, bappaji, tell me what should I do? I didn't even know he'd been gone six hours. Nobody told me till half an hour ago." Her voice was breaking.

"I am sorry, beti, to be bothering you at this time, but not knowing what happened is so much worse than ..." his voice was lost in the static. Then it came again, "Did you say you knew only now? That they told you only now?" Suddenly the old man's voice was tender, "Beti, beti, I am so sorry; take heart beti, and take care."

"Bappaji, I'll phone you when I find out, *pranam* mataji, pranam, bappaji."

She felt empty, better empty than give way to all the violence that was hammering at her heart. At least six hours had passed before Pritpal thought to phone her ... But Bappaji's voice had been so tender, so full of love, concern. She blocked away everything except their voices, bappaji, mataji, bappaji, mataji. How kind they had been when Niranjan had moved out. His mother had written a long letter, and she could see where tears had fallen and dried. One can never know what fate has ordained for us, bahu, and mother hearts imagine and fear all kinds of misfortune, but this, this we never, never had feared, never ... What can we say to you, bahu, what right any more do we have to say anything to you ... but please remember to ask if there is anything, anything at all we can do for you, remember our doors are always open for you, remember not to make us strangers to our grandsons, remember we are here for you, and our blessings go with you always ... Veeru had read the letter again and again, and it had helped drive away the anger, the jealousy, the hatred for a short time, a short time so she could sleep in that king-size bed which had been hers alone for almost a year since they had lain in it night after night.

To lose a son in a faraway land, never to even see his face before ... to lose a son. Her sons, how was she going to tell them? With the resilience of children, they had got out of the dismay and shock of having Niranjan move out, and they had grown; like her they had grown, and just when one thinks one had grown enough comes the winter wind ...

Not to know anything except that he was dead.

Veeru phoned Amy Wilkes, mother of Vikram's best friend, Eddie. Only a fence separated their yards. Seeing how close the boys were, they had cut a wicket gate in the fence last year.

"An emergency has come up, Amy," she said, "Could you please get the boys to your place after school. I have to go out."

"Sure, Veeru, can I help with anything?" Helpful but discreet as always. If she could not confide in Amy, what was neighbourliness all about?

"It would help if you walked to the school and came back with them, so they don't come home? I don't want them to come home."

"Sure, Veeru." Curiosity, naturally. Why not a simple note on the door as usual, telling them to go to Eddie's?

"Amy, I've had some bad news. About their father ... I am going out to find out ..."

"I am sorry to hear that, Veeru. Don't worry about the boys. I'll keep them till you call again. Don't worry about a thing. Just do what you have to."

Sweet Amy. If only I knew what it is I have to do.

She sat by the telephone, expecting it to ring. But it did not ring. The house was big and quiet. The ghosts started moving. And still no call. From the party workers, there was no word, except for that one phone call from Pritpal. They were too busy doing what had to be done, Veeru thought. They knew what they had to do. The staircase started swaying. It was a beautiful staircase, with a wide even arc that started in the middle of the living room and swung up over the dining room and reached towards the skylight above the open area around which were the bedrooms. When Veeru came with the two boys to set up house, Niranjan had already moved here from his old apartment. At first she was disappointed at the lack of carpets and marble tiles, but that would come after, she consoled herself. It was only in the last two years, since Niranjan had moved out and she had started working, that she knew how classy this house was. She had caught on fast to much of what real estate as business meant; she now knew the cultural differences between houses with marble-tiled bathrooms and saunas, and houses with hardwood floors and oak bannisters. She knew how to distinguish between types of clientele. Niranjan, with his moneyed background and Canadian education knew what was what. This was a beautiful, upper class house, smaller than those in which most Indians lived, but impeccably designed and renovated.

Veeru looked at the crystal chandeliers, not gaudy and huge but dainty; at the neat hardwood floor, the parquet in the hallways, the way the squares fitted just right, the way the walls curved off the living room and hallways ... She kept her mind busy on all the details of architecture and decor to block out the silent dragging steps of the ghosts that moved around her. And she waited for the phone to ring. At last there was a bell, the front door chime. She had left it open, not intentionally. Rahim came in and they met halfway. And with him came her tears. They held each other and cried, except that he knows what he is crying for, Veeru thought, drawing away.

She asked him to phone Bappaji. They would still be waiting, poor old parents, to lose a son in a faraway land ... From listening to Rahim's call, she found out what had happened. They were driving back from Nelson. Two carloads. Rahim was driving his car just a little behind

Niranjan. Just past midnight. A drunk driver in a half ton smashed right into the driver's side. Not a scratch on the half ton. No one else seriously injured. Death had been instantaneous: DOA — dead on arrival — is what the certificate read. The cremation? Oh he didn't know. There were so many things to be done. He had been taken to Gardiner Funeral Home around two. Not tonight or tomorrow. That's how things are in this country ... The party needed time to honour him. Workers were coming from all over the province, even from Alberta, and so the weekend was a better time ... Yes, Chachaji, I know how you feel about our people's custom to cremate the same day ... no, how can it be an abomination to take the time to honour him ... Chachaji, he was our leader, our Bhai Sahib, we owed him so much, we owe him a public funeral, Chachaji, your son was everything to us ... Jitin? He had left her just half an hour ago, the baby was okay, yes, there were enough of them to take care of her. Veeru? Yes, yes, he was with her: they would make sure she was not alone, yes, of course. The boys were with a neighbour, no they had not yet been told, yes, they would. Yes, they would make sure Veeru was okay, yes.

There was a long pause as Rahim listened and said nothing. And then he responded again. "Yes, it is a grievous omission on our part, Chachaji, things just happened too fast ... I beg your forgiveness, Chachaji, and hers too, yes, hers, I shall never forgive myself, I didn't know, I just assumed ... things happened so fast, so many of us, each thought ... I know, no excuse, no excuse at all ... I hold your feet and beg your pardon, Chachaji, and hers too, yes, hers."

He placed the receiver back in its cradle and fell at Veeru's feet, held on to her feet and cried, and she knew why.

"The boys have to be told. I'd better call them back," she said. "You might as well leave, Rahim, once the boys come, we'll manage. Have something to drink."

"I am staying here" he said, going to the phone. Once he started speaking, he figured he should use the dining room phone; he laid the receiver down and went to the dining room. Veeru heard voices being raised within moments of Rahim saying hello. "No, I am not coming anywhere. I am busy, and am going to be busy the rest of the evening." Through the receiver he had left in the living room, she could hear the other person cursing him. What do you mean, Shit, they need you here, have you forgotten you have to bring ... I am not coming back, get that, NOT Coming Back ... Shit, are you getting drunk at some pub, get your butt here ... And what if I was getting drunk? What Christly business is it of yours, I'll get as boozed as I damn well please ...

Rahim did not come back to the living room.

Veeru's eyes filled with tears. Rahim, sweet, sweet Rahim. She could not remember when she had last seen him: she had completely dropped out of that world. This morning if anyone had asked her if she missed that world, she'd have said, No way, I don't know how or why I put up with it so long. The last two years had been exciting; she had grown, had adeptly learnt the ropes and greatly enjoyed her rise in the profession. She had made full use of their membership at Glencoe Club that they had seldom used in all those years. She had learnt to dress up and explore all that the club offered, including entry into a different class of business.

But Rahim, who brought her stolen flowers every time he visited them in those early days, sweet Rahim made her ache for all those years that had been erased by Niranjan sitting on the bed and telling her he would phone her doctor the next day. That's what had set going the downward spiral of their lives, no, his life, she corrected herself, and now he had tumbled down the last step. The wastefulness of it all, he still had so much to do, the labour of years was starting to bear fruit ....oh the wastefulness of it all.

She was glad Rahim was going to stay, even if it was something that he had to be told from ten thousand miles away. Bappaji, mataji, their voices soothing her from halfway around the world, to lose a son in a faraway land ...

Their grief assuaged hers somewhat, blocked out her aloneness, the heavy weight of how no one had called. The workers. She had never been part of their world then? Was that it? Like a stone ingested by some willy-nilly act of misplaced idealism, housed for a time, cast out along with other products the body did not need, the party did not need. She would show them, show them she could stand on her own, she and her sons, *her* sons, not his any more. She would show them.

She phoned Amy. The boys had had their dinner with them, Amy said, and they were doing their homework: would it be okay to send them in, say, half an hour? If you could please walk them over, Amy. Of course, sure.

She waited at the kitchen window, so she could see them coming through the wicket they had made in their fence. Her sons, how beautiful they were! Both had her face, round and soft, with no cheekbones or angles, and her head of black thick hair. But Vikram was already a teenager, and in a growing spurt. He looked exactly the way she remembered her brothers; how are they now, she wondered, how rarely she got around to writing to them, oh how we drift away from old bonds, the only bonds that really hold, and Bappaji's tender voice held her up as she watched her sons walk towards her. She asked Rahim to tell Amy the news after she'd brought the boys in, and to stay outside for a while.

The boys knew something was wrong. Amy had let them believe it was news from India. Veeru sat them on the sofa and knelt in front of them. Daddy's had an accident, she said. She held her palms up on their knees, an old family ritual. Any time either parent had to announce a decision or compromise, they would hold their hands up, and the boys would place one of their hands palm down on the parent's and listen. Then they would clasp and do their part. It was the final step of any argument they had as to who would do what chore, give up an afternoon party with school friends in order to be together as a family at some other social commitment, whatever the issue, at this point it was a decision handed out that they must accept. And Adarsh always sat to his older brother's left, so that it was always Vikram's right hand she held and Adarsh's left. All that she had visualized as she'd waited for them to come home. But the words she had not, and they came stuttering out unthought.

"Daddy was in an accident last night, and he is ..." she paused, gone to heaven? no, even Adarsh had grown out of that surely, we have bad news? they knew that already ... "dead." Adarsh's hand clutched hers but Vikram's was inert.

"Without even saying goodbye?" Adarsh asked.

"There was no time, sweetheart, he was on his way back from Nelson. But he said goodbye in his heart, for sure he did, you were right there, centre field in his heart, and Vikram too."

"And the baby?"

Veeru sighed. "Yes, of course, the baby too, all of us." Vikram's hand pressed hers. He hated them, Jitin for sure, perhaps the baby too. And he did not want them there in the centre field of his father's heart even in his last moments.

"We will go say goodbye to him, maybe tomorrow morning?" she said.

Vikram's hand said, "No." Or was it hers?

"Who is he? He stinks, I mean literally, like he hasn't had a bath in years."

"Vik, that is Rahim, one of our oldest friends, my oldest friend," how quickly she had picked up what Vikram needed to hear, hers not his father's. "He was the first, almost the first, person I met when I first came to Canada. He was a boy then, only a few years older than you are now. He has always been my good friend."

"How come I don't know him then?"

"Why can't we see him now?"

It was easier to answer Adarsh. "It is already night, sweetheart. Daddy is at the funeral home. Let us go to bed early. And we'll sleep in the big bed tonight."

Adarsh's hand tightened. He would like that. But Vikram drew away his hand; he would have none of it. "I'll sleep in my own bed," he said through his teeth. And he got up and stormed upstairs, slamming the door of his room.

"Where is Daddy? Is he all right, alone?"

And Veeru's heart tightened with grief. Where would he be? Alone in some dreadful drawer in the funeral home? Or being dolled up by some skilled mortician rising to the challenge of putting pieces together? I am with you, love, you are not alone.

But even grief always turns to anger — he was not alone, he was perhaps at home, with party workers thronging the place, consoling her, the baby handled from lap to lap, both safe, safe in the arms and tears of friends. If such anger could flow from Vikram to her, it could flow from her to Adarsh, and that must not be. Or was it that it was coming from her, and Vikram could sense it?

She took Adarsh to the kitchen and gave him his usual glass of milk with a cookie. I don't think I want this, he said. I want Daddy. She hugged him. It is always good to keep to one's routine when bad things happen, she said, it helps you a lot, trust me, sweetheart. How about if I whip it up with marshmallow Quik?

She went to Rahim who was lying on the couch in the family room. He asked if he should talk to Vikram. She said no, no, she would bring him around. Rahim had heard the slamming door but he did not know that Vikram hated him too. "Rahim, please do help yourself to something from the fridge. I am not up to it but I'd be upset if you don't take care of yourself; this is a bedsitter, I guess you know how it opens out? You know, there is a bathroom here." She took out pillows, sheets, towels, etc. Then she went upstairs.

Adarsh was in his pyjamas in his room, staring at his father's photograph, the only one in the house these two years. I love you, Daddy. How many times she had heard him say those words these two years ...? Her heart tightened with pain for this little boy who looked so much like her at his age, but he was not the one whom she had to worry about. He never had been. It was Vikram, with all that turmoil held back inside.

She went to his room, and knelt by his bed, where he lay in the fetal position, facing the wall. She reached out and put her face on his back, which instantly went rigid. She whispered, "I need both of you near me," she said. "Especially you, sweetheart Vik, I have been so alone all day." And her voice broke, because the violence came hammering again. Alone, how could they have let her be alone all day?

"That guy was with you." Jealousy. She had perhaps overdone it about Rahim having been the first person she'd met, etc. "No, he came by only after four; and I was glad to see him, see someone, anyone. I didn't know what to do. I was not ready for Addu and so I phoned Amy. I wanted you to come home rightaway but didn't know how. What are we going to do, sweetheart?"

They were silent a long time.

"I hate him," Vikram said with bottled up venom. "I don't want to see him." Several times each week the boys had spent time with Niranjan and all of them had seemed to be coming to a measure of stability, so Vikram's violent outburst stunned her. From her to him? God, god, this shouldn't be.

"It is okay to hate him for having left us, yes, even for dying ..." she said slowly, "it is okay to hate, but only for a short time, sweetheart. Hate him tonight for dying on us, but tomorrow, maybe not tomorrow, but soon, remember him for all those other years. I can't leave Addu alone, come we'll talk there."

But he would not move. So she went to Addu and lay in the big bed until he fell asleep. Then she went again to her older son. And talked and talked and thus soothed him and herself. At one point, he said with violent clenched teeth, "I hate her. I hate her." And she heard herself saying, "No, Vik, you must never hate a woman; hate your father, hate any man you want to, for a short time, for a short time it is okay to hate a man, but never a woman. You must never hate a woman, no matter what."

"That is what you've always said, Mom, telling us all women are special, special, what is so special about someone like that, a home-breaker."

"I spoke to Bappaji and Mataji today," she said. "They think so too. I think that's how they see her, as someone who took their son away from us. I understand them, Vik. That's the way the older generation thinks and feels, that women somehow are to blame. My mother, my own mother, thought I was to blame for Daddy leaving us. That is how we have been taught for centuries — to think that women are to blame when something goes wrong. You know I was not to blame and you must believe that Jitin Aunty (she almost couldn't say the name but Vikram had to relearn to say it, he had to) is not to blame for anything that has happened."

That left Niranjan. But she let it be. It is all right to hate someone, as long as it is only for a short time.

"So it is all right to hate Daddy."

"Yes, he is a man, he can take it, sweetheart, it is all right to hate him tonight for leaving us, for dying on us, for all the mess of our lives ... but only for a short time, not tomorrow maybe but soon, we are going to straighten out the mess and go back to ..." could she say the words? she had to, Vikram had to hear them said, "loving him."

"I don't want to see him."

She didn't either. For Adarsh's sake, they would go to him, the three of them hand-in-hand, and bid him goodbye. Just the three of them, privately, and leave the workers to their hoopla. From the little that Rahim had told Bappaji, there was to be a big funeral. To her he had not said anything and she had not asked, waiting for him to speak. Rahim. The memory of those early days had made her cling to him, but Vikram was right. Rahim, this almost thirty-year-old man she had not seen in years, was here because his leader's father had ordered him from halfway around the world to stay with his son's wife. Veeru lay still, thinking. Sadly, and with glee? There must be another word for it. For them, she, Veeru, was their daughter-in-law, not that faceless woman with whom their son had been living. Jitin, Jitin, she thought longingly, remembering the comfort of her arms which she could not now return, when Jitin needed comfort. No, Jitin did not need her, surrounded as she surely was with people who worshipped her the way they had worshipped him. She had never needed her.

Later that night, when Adarsh had a nightmare and shouted for Daddy, it was Vikram, who had quietly taken his father's place on the other side of his brother in the bed, who took charge and soothed him back to sleep.

The newspaper carried a short obit with a photograph.

The phone rang all day.

Vikram had his arm around his brother's shoulder as they went to school.

There was a knock on the door and then the doorbell buzzed, it was DHL Courier Service. Veeru signed for a cardboard carton from Toronto. She opened the envelope taped to the top. On Air India letterhead was the message:

> Dear Mrs. Anand,
>
> As requested by Captain Pravin Vohra, we send you herewith this package.

She opened the carton. Packed in layers and layers of plastic and newspaper were a bottle of water, an envelope with two flat paper packets — sacred ash and sindoor, and a letter. It was from Bappaji.

> Dear daughter Veeru,
>
> We have little right to ask you for anything, and no right at all to tell you what you should do. And yet, if you will, please get Vikram to place a drop of Gangajal on his father's lips. We cannot forget what our son took away from the young boys, but let them not keep from him the cleansing waters of the Ganga, or themselves from their inheritance. They are his sons, as he was mine: this is our inheritance, their inheritance.

*****

Saturday morning Veeru and the boys went to the funeral chapel for their private farewell. Sharmaji was there, dressed in his priest's clothes, Indian shirt and pants of khadi silk, silk scarf on his shoulder. Vikram was calm, like a full-grown man, she thought, the man of the house, oh my darling, don't leave childhood behind so soon. In his black achkan and white chudidars, he looked taller and older than his thirteen years. While little Adarsh solemnly looked at the open casket, Vikram under Sharmaji's tutelage placed tilak and sacred ash on his father's forehead, and sprinkled Gangajal on his eyelids and lips. Sharmaji's rich voice enunciated slokas sanctified over time, and then they played a tape of "Raghupati Raghava Raja Ram." All three of them knelt next to the casket and listened to the song.

"I love you, Daddy," Adarsh, too solemn for tears, repeated it like a mantra. "I love you, Daddy." Veeru did not dare hope that Vikram would say or do anything more, but he did. After they rose, he touched his father's feet with both hands then raised his hands to his head. An age-old gesture he had been coached in, when barely three, by his grandparents both in the village and in Delhi, came back to him. Veeru silently raised her voice in thanks that he had accepted his inheritance.

He came into a greater inheritance at the funeral later that afternoon. Veeru became thankful for Bappaji's message from halfway around the world that they should be there.

The hall was filled to capacity, there were people standing in the aisles, all the way to the altar and back to the foyer door. Veeru chose the tenth row, far enough from the front that no one should notice them, and near the centre aisle. The line was endless: mourners walked up the left aisle, each stood a moment at the now closed casket, then walked down the right aisle. The casket was draped with a hammer and sickle flag, a sight that must have startled some of those from the university and government, even though Niranjan's leftist leanings were often in the news.

It seemed the entire fruit belt had turned up, or at least one person from each generation of every Sikh family who lived and worked there. They came, old men with white beards, old women prematurely grey but with sturdy peasant bodies, young men who had carried Boss's message all over the province. At one point there seemed to be a little scuffle when a group of yellow-clad turbaned men each wearing a very visible and very outsize sword demanded that the lid be raised so they could salute their leader, but between Sharmaji and the gurdwara priest, the men were pacified. They stood on either side of the casket, canopying it with their unsheathed swords, and sang a hymn that resounded off the high ceiling. Adarsh to her right, tightened his grasp on her hand and Vikram, to her left, slid his hand into hers. Instead of walking down the right aisle, the men walked down the centre aisle, and stopped next to Vikram. One of them placed his hand on his heart and boomed, "Veer Shahid, Amar Shahid, may his sons live forever." Veeru thought they meant it in a general way, but then all of them bowed to Vikram and repeated the gesture and words. "Veer Shahid, Amar Shahid, may his sons live forever." Once again, Vikram rose to the occasion. He stood up, bowed his head and greeted them with joined palms, with one gesture both accepting their tribute and asking their blessing. The chapel's security men, who had discreetly raced to the scene, relaxed.

A few minutes later, with the line still winding around the flag-draped coffin, Jitin came in, a group of women behind her, through one of the side doors behind. Veeru had been looking for her; she had half expected that Jitin, being Jitin, would appear in the same line as all the rest and would then slip into the front row. Because all her thoughts were on Jitin, she would have spotted her rightaway, no matter from which direction she came. Even though she was silently crying out all the time for Jitin, when she actually saw her, she felt as though she had suddenly been clubbed. Her heart was ready to burst in an implosion of grief. Jitin stood in the doorway, all in white, her dupatta draped over her head, her face pale, dry, and utterly beautiful. She held the baby in her arms and she stood in the doorway, waiting, while the last of the line wound its way past the casket.

Veeru wanted to rush down and embrace her and never let her go. A great sob rose in her throat and she wanted to cry the way women cried back home at funerals, long ululating cries that would staunch welling, swelling hearts from imploding. Jitin, Jitin, Jitin. She shook her hands free from Vikram and Adarsh, and half rose. But just then the baby whimpered, and the women enclosed Jitin: one took the baby from Jitin's arms, one helped her readjust her dupatta, another conjured up a glass of water for her to drink. Veeru sat down, took Vikram's hand and whispered, "Hold my hand, Vik, don't let go of my hand, ever."

The service was like nothing anyone had ever attended and it was in every newspaper the next day. It was like a military funeral in its precision. At least twenty men and women spoke but each was clear and brief, and no one seemed to repeat what anyone else had said about Niranjan's work. Some spoke in Hindi, some in Punjabi and some in English, but all were passionate in their praise and grief. Then a choir, that had come all the way by chartered bus from Edmonton, sang "The International."

It was enthralling, now like being in some heavenly hall, now like being in open fields, now rowing across a blue lake with a hundred thousand suns shining on the shimmering water.

> Toilers from shops and fields united,
> The party we of all who work;
> The earth belongs to us, the people,
> No room here for the shirk.
>
> Tis the final conflict,
> Let each stand in his place,
> The international party
> Shall be the human race.

Vikram's eyes were shining with the light of his inheritance. Their leader, their hero, was his father, whom one day he would learn to love.

*****

The lawyer explained it patiently to her. The will, written five years ago, was valid only if some other will did not turn up. According to Niranjan's insurance policy, his daughter by Jitin was his beneficiary but Veeru by default was the sole inheritor of all other assets, if no other will turned up. However, his present wife was entitled to contest the will. There would be a lot of paperwork to be done by her since the divorce papers had been filed in India and not here: moreover, the second wedding had not been registered. However, it was performed in a local gurdwara and it would not be difficult for the present wife to get the papers. That neither of them was a Sikh could be looked into, but it was unlikely the court would question its validity. In short, she should start thinking about how she would like him to negotiate the terms.

But Jitin did not come forward with another will nor did she contest the will. She did not hire a lawyer. She just came in, carefully read whatever Veeru's lawyer gave her and signed where he asked her to.

*****

From time to time, Bimla fed her information about Jitin. Bimla was a gossip. Veeru did not trust her but she was nevertheless Veeru's friend. She had a husband in some clerical job in some government office, and he always came to the concerts and parties walking half a step behind his wife: she clearly was the leader of the team.

Bimla was always there for her, somewhat fawning, somewhat bossy, but always available. She spent Veeru's money freely, but it was convenient to have someone to go out with, and someone who would run errands and do some odds and ends to keep the house running, all the little things in the house that had to be to attended to. Veeru had only to phone Bimla about a faucet leak or a door that had jammed or a broken window pane and Bimla would do the rest; Veeru guessed that Bimla got some kind of cut, not in cash but in trade-offs from the various workmen, always Punjabi, that she brought in.

Bimla gave her titbits about people that she thought Veeru would like to hear, and bad news about Jitin was something she assumed

Veeru would like to hear. So through the last five years, Veeru heard about how sickly little Niranjana was, how once she almost died of dehydration, how Jitin had gone part-time on her job so she could stay home more. And now, Bimla came to tell her about the year's Solidarity Day bhangra. It was called that but it had been Boss's birthday that had started it one year. It had become an annual festival where music and beer flowed freely and they danced through the night. Bimla, as always, had news of Jitin. The school had laid her off at the end of the last term. They could not put up with her overuse of sick leave to take care of her child. She was now working in Mandeep Grocery Store three times a week, and somewhere else for two days. Manbhai was a good man and Jitin could work as many or as few hours as she pleased, but he was not so good that he would pay her a good wage. Minimum wage was probably what she was getting, Bimla said.

Veeru was shocked to hear about the layoff from the school division. Jitin could surely appeal to the union, why hadn't she?

Bimla shrugged with some contempt. "You know how she is, doesn't know the first thing about claiming her rights. Sets up unions everywhere for everyone else yet not thinking of herself." Veeru did not say anything. Anytime Bimla talked about Jitin's simplicity, Veeru felt Bimla was targeting her for her part in the estate settlement that had kept the community buzzing for months. Some had talked about Jitin's naiveté in not contesting the will, others about Veeru's callousness in cutting her off without a cent, but the whole thing blew over, with the general consensus being that somehow justice had been served. Jitin had Niranjan and Veeru had the rest of his money — all was fair. Each lived exactly as they had heretofore, so why should others complain? they said. The party workers staunchly stood by Jitin: Boss had been above filthy lucre and of course Jitin was too.

But soon after that, the party had gone in quite another direction, under a new leader who knew how to channel government funds their way. The party now had an office, and an executive director, and operating funds from various departments of the government. It had changed its name, and its manifesto was now called a Constitution, its Working Party was known as the Board, it was registered as a non-profit ethnic organization, and was a member of the national Intercultural Council. Within two years, it had become even more of a force in the province. Politicians now came to their events wearing coloured turbans, with wives in colourful salwar-kameez, and they all clapped to bhangra music and drank Taj beer imported from Delhi.

One Friday afternoon, Veeru set off. She knew what she had to do. She had to persuade Jitin to take a fair share of the assets. She had thought of getting her lawyer to draw up something, but then knew Jitin would simply refuse to sign just as she had simply signed without a question the last time. Vikram was playing Junior League hockey. Adarsh, faithful fan, would be there. And Amy, sweet Amy Wilkes, she would pick them at the arena after the game.

Veeru parked her car in the Mall Parkade and walked down Jubilee Avenue. She did not care to park her Audi on the street, at the end of which was the junior high school. She had not driven the Volvo since after the accident. Even as she had heard Pritpal's incoherent voice that day, her mind had zeroed in on how Niranjan had insisted on leaving her the Volvo and taken the Tercel. In the years they were together, he had always taken the Volvo for out-of-town trips, but when he moved, he had left it with her: the boys had to be safe and so she must have the safer car. There, too, he had made the decision despite her demurring. Nevertheless, she felt remorse, guilt, so she'd bought an Audi. The Volvo was still there, unused, covered with tarpaulin. Soon after the funeral, when she had decided to sell it, Vikram had been adamant. He wanted it, his inheritance, his new-found allegiance to his father. Vikram got his licence the day after his sixteenth birthday and a day late only because his birthday fell on a Sunday. He was waiting for the Christmas break to fix the Volvo and take it over.

School was just out. Veeru wished she had worn her usual skirt outfit instead of a sari, it was a Mysore chiffon, and as always, she wore expensive matching accessories. In this district, it looked quite out of place. She instantly realized how much she had changed, how prejudiced she had become.

She turned onto Croft Street and was overcome with sadness. The house was exactly the same as it had been ten years ago, the garage still somewhat teetering, the window frames still peeling paint, and the flowers still bright and wild all along the house.

Just ahead of her on the sidewalk was a teenager holding a little girl's hand. Both were singing a nursery rhyme. They opened the wicket. The teenager, a white girl, took out a key and let themselves in the house. Bimla had told her that at some point Niranjan had bought the house and had the party's office upstairs.

Veeru followed them and rang the bell. The little girl peeked out the screen door and said, "Some aunty is here, Katie, come open the door." Katie came to the door, and opened it with a smile. Veeru realized that her sari was the reason for the open door. She was glad she had not worn her office clothes after all: a tailored suit, however expensive, would not have had the Open Sesame effect that her sari had.

"I seem to have come too early," Veeru said glibly giving the girl the impression that she was expected. "I thought Jitin would be home by now."

"She'll be home in about half an hour, an hour at most. Would you like to wait?"

Katie invited her in. She introduced herself as the babysitter who took charge of Nira for an hour, bringing her home from the day-care on weekday afternoons. She took Niranjana by the hand and said firmly, "You, kiddo, can talk to the lady only after your fruit and yoghurt." They went off to the kitchen.

Veeru looked around the room. It was awfully small and closed in. How airy and large her apartment upstairs had been, she thought, or was she feeling cramped only because of her present house? No, the ground floor was indeed small. The staircase and landing were spacious, she remembered, with a closet at the base where the workers used to store bicycles and shoes and raincoats those weekends they worked at a feverish pitch to get some workshop going. No wonder the main floor was so small. Also, the trees and houses on either side made it dark. The linoleum on the hall floor to the kitchen was old and cracked, but the center of the room was familiar: the Kashmiri silk carpet, the walnut coffee tables, the stereo and television systems, all were still there. And the couch. Tears sprang to her eyes. The couch: Niranjan had brought it literally from someone's else's garbage one morning during her first trip that summer of 1982. It was solid oak, with sturdy slats, wide arms and no cushions. "Crazy people," he had said, "they are throwing this away and probably replacing it with some hardboard junk covered with expensive upholstery." It was heavy, but he seemed to have had no problem heaving it to their steps. Then he had got help — was it Rahim? — to haul it upstairs. She had selected the new fabric. She remembered how he had stood shaking his head dubiously in the store, "sure you want something with turquoise circles?" he had asked, and she had said, "but of course I do, they are such small circles and they will brighten up the room, just you wait and see."

How often that summer they had lain there, ostensibly watching some television show, she in the curve of his arm ...

Veeru heard a door bang but it was the door to the upstairs. With a shock, she realized that Jitin had probably rented out the rooms upstairs. It jolted her — this state of destitution. She felt the old anger rise again: how irresponsible of him, how careless, inconsiderate of him to leave them in this state.

"My name is Nira," she heard, "what is yours, aunty?"

Veeru turned and saw the child directly for the first time, and tears sprung again. Vikram, she thought, so like Vikram at that age, his father's little bright eyes, and shock of soft black hair, the same nose, the same way the hair fell over the ears. Vikram was now more like her, his face round, his hair thick and curly, but at that age how his grandparents and aunts had doted on him, spitting image of his father ... She felt weak with nostalgia for that sprawling house in Safdarjang where her real adult life had started. Bappaji, Mataji.

"I love your sari," she said, feeling Veeru's sari. Veeru picked her up. So light, so small, like a feather that would blow away; she placed her lips against the child's forehead and the child in turn dutifully pecked her on the cheek. She must be used to being picked up by strangers, Veeru thought, so unafraid, so uninhibited. She remembered the baby being passed from hand to hand at the church, while Addu had refused to let go of her hand even a moment so she could quietly wipe away her tears.

"My name is Niranjana," she said, again, "but everyone calls me Nira." Veeru remembered hearing how the original name Ranjana had been changed after her father's death to Niranjana.

"My name is Veerbala, but everyone calls me Veeru."

"My mom's name is Jitender, but everyone calls her Jitin Aunty."

It became a game. "Katie's name is Katherine, but everyone calls her Katie."

"I have two boys at home. One's name is Vikram, but everyone calls him Vik."

"And the other?"

"His name is Adarsh, and nowadays everyone calls him Adarsh."

They laughed together. "Let us give him some other name."

"No, he wouldn't like that."

"Mom sometimes calls me 'little monkey'."

"Do you like that name?"

"Only when Mom calls me by it."

"Yes, moms can call their babies anything in the world, can't they? Oh I almost forgot, I've brought you something." Veeru took out the wrapped gift from her bag.

"For me?"

"Yes, for you."

"Did you know I'd be here when you came to see Mom?"

"Yes, I knew I'd find the sweetest little girl in the world in this house."

Nira carefully unwrapped the gift, a book. "Thank you, Veeru Aunty," she said, clearly taught to be polite. When she opened the book, however, the squeal of delight was genuine. It was an ABC book but with pop-up pictures on every page, elaborately folded so that layers and angles popped-up on every page. Veeru turned the page to M, and there popped a monkey on a tree branch. Ooh!

Veeru smiled. The two little faces did look alike, little bright eyes under protruding lids, a pug nose, a little thin face, and Veeru remembered the monkeys in her village, Hanuman monkeys they were called because they had long tails: how soft their grey fur was, and how beady and bright their eyes as they naughtily nibbled at bananas stolen from trees. But this child was so small, so light, like a wisp of cotton fluff that would disappear. Veeru held her like a paper doll, remembering how chubby Addu had been, how she could press her face hard against his tummy, his arms, his cheeks and feel the rolls of baby fat while he thumped her on her head in glee.

Katie, unable to check her curiosity, joined them on the couch. They hardly noticed the door opening, but almost at once Nira started sneezing. Jitin came in, bringing with her an aroma of cumin and coriander and chili powders from the store. Nira shouted, "Mom, look we have a new aunty!" And she sneezed nonstop. Jitin came in, and hurriedly said, "I'll be back in a minute. Niru's allergies act up and won't stop until I have my shower. Thank you, Katie dear, I guess you don't have to wait any longer. See you Monday." She disappeared into the bedroom, almost as though she had not recognized Veeru, and yet assuming she would take charge of the child.

Katie said her goodbyes and left. Nira continued to sneeze. Veeru carried her out into the yard, wondering if the flowers too would affect the poor child. She was so frail, so small, like a feather, oh my god, what Jitin must have gone through to bring her even to this state of normalcy. Four wasted years, she thought, God, where have I been? What have I become?

"Tell me a story," Nira said, laying her head on Veeru's shoulder.

"What story would you like?"

"A new one, about a monkey."

Veeru started the story of the monkeys and the cap-seller, pausing after every sentence to see if Nira knew the story already, but she didn't. Her hums became softer and then stopped altogether. She was fast asleep. Veeru carried her in and laid her in the recliner next to the couch, which Jitin must have prepared after they'd had gone outside: there was now a little pillow and a flannelette blanket, and the ottoman placed just right to make it longer. Veeru sat on the edge of the couch, and watched the long lashes, the little round mouth, incredibly soft hair, the finger of one thin hand in her mouth and the other hand on the new book that seemed huge next to her. So fragile, like everything between us.

Veeru thought of Jitin with the same longing as ever, that had not lost its edge of pain, that would never lose that edge of pain no matter how many years passed. Jitin, Jitin, her heart cried, the smell of masalas and condiments lingering in her mind.

Jitin came in, her hair washed and still wet, wearing a cotton kaftan that hung loosely on a body whose contours showed against the window. "So nice to see you, Veeru." Jitin went to Nira, drew her hand out of her mouth, blew her a kiss and said, "She always has a little nap while I get dinner ready. Poor child, I thought she was getting over her allergies but then I didn't know she would be so allergic to masalas until I started this job. Let me get us some tea." She paused and then turned.

Veeru saw her moving towards her as in slow motion from the stars. She felt her head drawn to the waiting breast, felt arms around her shoulders, tight, head pressed on her own, and heard Jitin's heart throbbing wildly. When the throbs turned from beats to rhythmic pulse, Jitin said, "Thank you for coming," and then, "How many nights I have lulled myself to sleep like this, Veeru, how many days I have imagined holding you just so when I've felt the ground sinking under me."

And then time stopped still.

Jitin held Veeru and gently ran her fingers over the outline of her hairline, gently, gently. Veeru trembled with remembrance: it was Niranjan's habit to do this, to her hands, her feet, stretching, curving each finger, each toe, running his fingers over the outline of her face like a blind man feeling every curl, every curve, tenderly, so tenderly. She could feel his lips on the nape of her neck, little pecks all the way down her arms to the tips of her fingers. How did she know, Veeru thought, but then how could she not know? She remembered his tongue licking, gently sucking, her nipples. But, no, that was long ago and even this perhaps was not really happening. Jitin raised Veeru's fingers to her lips. "Thank you for coming," she said again. "Thank you, god, thank you." They were silent and at peace.

The clock on the old firehall struck the half hour. Then Jitin drew away. "I haven't even made tea yet, come." But Veeru pulled her back. Then they clung to each other in a frenzy of need: hands, faces, mouths reaching out, the thirst of years seeking to be slaked. Jitin, Jitin, she moaned, and heard, love, love, my sweet love, and she did not know whether the voice she heard was real or in her head, his voice for surely the words were his, or hers, but it didn't matter, at last at last at last they were together.

They lay curved front to back, Jitin tracing her finger along the outline of Veeru's face, Veeru running her lips over the fingers of Jitin's other hand. One of them laughed, and then the other. They laughed together in little peals of suppressed chuckles.

"This is crazy," she said.

"If there be paradise on earth, it is this, it is this," said the other. Both fell silent in remembrance of other times, the other voice, romantically deep and rich, Urdu words like fresh spray from a rainbowed waterfall.

"I feel dizzy," she said.

"Like after chukkars," said the other, remembering the girlhood game of holding crossed hands with each other and spinning on their heels till their heads reeled to the sky.

They laughed. And lay still savouring the touch of arm on arm. And they laughed.

"This is crazy," she said.

"This is not the way I thought it would be," said the other.

"We are supposed to be serious, weepy."

"Not grinning."

"Passionate."

"Whoa, I thought we were. Ouch, I'll get you for that."

"Guilty."

"Furtive."

"Not laughing."

"No, we are doing it all wrong."

"One of us is supposed to be dying,"

"And the other comes."

"And they weep together."

"And the dying one takes the other's hands."

"Feebly, she is dying, remember?"

"And says, I leave my children in your care."

"And she dies."

"And the other cries heartbrokenly."

"And wants to kill herself."

"But one of the children comes in."

"And she clasps him to her bosom and promises she will live."

"Do you think we are crazy?"

"For being together like this?"

"No, stupid, for having wasted all these years."

"We have a lot of living to do."

"And laughing."

"I've never heard you laugh like this."

"I've never been as happy as this."

"I used to laugh a lot, remember?"

"Yes, I loved you for that."

"I must have been really stupid."

"For not knowing I was already there when you came?"

"No, stupid, for not knowing you loved me."

"We have a lot of living to do."

"And a lot of loving."

"How could you not have known?"

"What? That you were there before me?"

"No, stupid, that I was obsessed with you."

"Is that why you took him away from me?"

"That is different."

"Like he has nothing to do with all this?"

"Let us not talk about that."

"You loved him."

"Didn't you?"

"Not after he aborted my child."

"Did he? When? Why?"

"Didn't he tell you?"

"No, when was this?"

"Never mind."

"No, tell me."

"No."

"I am sorry, oh my love, I am sorry."

"It is over. I know I can love him now."

"You do?"

"Yes, now that I have you, I can love him again."

"You always had me."

"Why didn't you tell me, stupid?"

"I thought you would know. People are supposed to know these things."

"Stupid."

"Stupid."

"Stupid me."

"Stupid us."

"I think I am pretty smart, coming here today."

"I think I am pretty lucky."

"I am luckier."

"Because I stole him from you?"

"You only took what was always yours."

"We knew, we always knew."

"What?"

"About us, about this."

"Yes, that last day, when I saw you walking down, all in white, with the baby in your arms, I wanted to embrace you and never let you go."

"If I had let go of your hand even a moment, I would not have survived that ... those terrible days, that emptiness, that all-engulfing void."

"But you had all those people."

"And you had no one."

"You knew that?"

"How could I not?"

"But you never came, never called."

"But I did not let go of your hand a moment."

"Nor I yours."

"For always."

"Do you think this will work?"

"Why shouldn't it?"

"It might be just an obsession; we've wanted this for so long, we are blowing everything way out of proportion."

"You are right; we are; let's have some tea."

"You're not supposed to agree."

"Aren't you thirsty?"

"Yes, and hungry. Yes, yes, yes."

"Yes."

"I don't know. This is paradise, but anything more, anything else, might be less."

"Why?"

"I don't know. I mean this is all I want, ever wanted, this, bedrock, anchor." She tightened the other's arm around her.

"Stone and steel? You are weird, my sweet love, you are weird."

"Your laugh makes me so happy."

"Yours always did."

"But tell me ..."

"What?"

"That this will work out."

"How can I tell you that?"

"Because."

"That's been the trouble all along, this assumption of yours that I know everything, have been everywhere."

"Haven't you?"

"There you go again, making assumptions, Deedi, I am so glad I have you here to teach me everything."

"You remember that first day?"

"I remember that day every time I hold my baby close to my heart and want to keep her safe from the cruelty of the world. How often I held you, sweet one, that first summer."

"Why didn't you ever do it for real?"

"Because all I wanted was to hold you in my arms and cry; I was so sure that somehow everything would turn out right for all of us, if I could do it, just hold you."

"Why didn't you?"

"I don't know. That's the way I am, I guess. And your thinking I was a know-it-all didn't help then or later. How could I cry my heart out on your shoulder when you thought I was some goddess come to earth? I could only wait for you to come to me. And then it was all over. I became a bloodsucking demoness."

"Bloodsucking, yes,"

"I'll get you for that."

"Don't tickle me, you ..."

"Bloodsucking?"

"But goddess still."

"No, I'm tired of being that to everyone. It was ridiculous, even hilarious, the way everyone in the party pretended I was a virgin."

"I love you when you laugh."

"Even though you drew your hand away just now?"

"You shouldn't be so damn observant."

"How you must have hated me!"

"Never. Never. You should have known."

"That day at that meeting, long ago, when I turned from the window you were looking at me, and I thought, Now, now my waiting is over."

"The domestic workers' steering committee ..."

"But you didn't look at me the rest of the afternoon."

"I was too busy trying to hate you."

"You had every right to. I am glad you did."

"Never. And because I couldn't hate you, I hated him."

"No, no, you didn't."

"Yes, yes, I hated him."

"Don't say it."

"I must, I can. Because I don't any more. I miss him, oh how I miss him, I want to say sorry for the way I strangled him, his love for me, my love for him."

"Hush, sweetest, hush."

But it was she who spoke of him again. "There were so many things he wanted to do, we wanted to do."

"You can start again. Please start again."

"All gone to dust even before his ashes reached the sea."

"No, don't say that. The old guard are there. They will come back. I am here. We'll get it all back. All."

"All?"

"Tell me, tell me this will last."

"Of course it will."

"That feels good."

"Words or hands?"

"Both. For now. But anything else will be less."

"Meaning?"

"Demands, expectations, all that one thinks one should be able to give and get: something happens when it is for real. Remember when we were girls, everything was so innocent, so pure, so beautiful."

"Rainbows."

"Yes, yes, rainbows. Did you also have this thing about rainbows?"

"Don't we all?"

"Was it always there for you, even after ..."

"Yes. Yes ... I'm sorry if it hurts you."

"It shouldn't ... You deserved to have all that was always yours."

"Maybe because it was always so short there was never time for the shine to wear off."

"You see what I mean? About this, about us."

"Savitri used to say, 'Never consummate your first love, and you will have it forever.'"

"So you agree."

"About what?"

"About this, that the only way we can keep it is by not going on together."

"You are afraid."

"Yes."

"So am I."

"You are not supposed to say that."

"I didn't say anything. You're dreaming."

"I don't want to wake up."

"God willing we won't."

"Who is Savitri?"

"Jealous?"

"I am right, ain't I?"

"I'd like to let on you are."

"You're devious."

"What else can you expect from a woman who steals your husband from under your nose?"

"It is so good to hear you laugh."

"It's growing dark."

"I grew so much, but it was never enough."

"You grew to be what you were born to be. It was wonderful, it was awesome, the way you spiralled out and away from our orbit."

"Alone. Always alone. And the more alone I was the more power I seemed to draw from god knows where. Vengefulness?"

"We'll never be alone again."

"God willing."

"This is paradise, but you do have to get up and go back to your children."

"Our children. Ours."

"To have and to hold."

"From this day forward."

"Till death do us part."

"Do you think we are crazy?"

"You maybe, but not me. Never."

"It is so wonderful to hear you laugh."

"We will laugh again, dance and sing."

"But tell me, aren't we being crazy? Like just-pubescent teenagers."

"I wouldn't know; I rose full-blown from the ocean."

"I thought I'd never see your smile again."

"You are going to see it morning, noon and night."

"I never thought you, we, could be so crazy."

"Never been saner."

"Never happier. Well, that isn't true. I was happy for a long time, and I wouldn't want to erase the past."

"Nor I."

"So you'd do it again?"

"I am sure."

"Steal my husband?"

"I loved him with my whole soul."

"I don't know if I was/am ever capable of loving anyone that way. But now I think I can love him again the way I used to."

"We are crazy."

"We are happy."

"We are going to be even happier."

"God willing."

"God has willed it so from the beginning."

"But we were too stupid to see or hear."

Maru and the M.M. Syndrome

One

Everything seemed to be in order but it was not yet twelve so I ran over the list of files on the hard drive again. I found one I had overlooked when moving old records onto floppies, good. I filed it away correctly. I opened the master file and went over the instructions I was leaving my successor. Everything was fine. Whoever she was to be, she'd know exactly what was where.

It was like any other day for all but me. Just about everyone knew I was going away on my annual vacation. Very few knew I was not coming back after that. Students came in with their usual requests that I stamp the date and time on their assignments. I love them, these young people with their smarmy attitudes and snide remarks about Prof. X who was never in his office during his consultation hours, Prof. Y whose marginal comments are totally illegible, Prof. Z who spends far too much time telling anecdotes ... Those who came to cadge off me always had the most happy smiles pasted on their face. "Maru, can I borrow your stapler, please?" "Maru, I need to run off just one copy on your copier, pretty please." I love them, these kids still wet behind the ears though others might say they are quite, quite insufferable. Oh, how I am going to miss them!

I am going to miss all this, I said to myself for the nth time. Fifteen years at this job, in three different departments, it is true, but the same job. One thing was sure, though, I will never say "I am going to miss you guys." I have had enough. It's the male faculty around here who were driving me up the wall.

This m.m. syndrome is frightening. Of course, one knows the basic symptoms of male menopause as well as one knows about hot flashes and mood swings in women, though television talk shows never parade men the way they do women. We secretaries know a lot about these things: not just about our own husbands and fathers and brothers and neighbours but the ten or fifteen men that each of us works with everyday, and some of the women faculty who could just as well be men. In our collective wisdom, we share our knowledge over lunch: it is a quite formidable database.

The stories we could tell! But of course we won't. We are secretaries, souls of discretion, loaded with all the confidential files on all the faculty members of this university, not all of which are on floppies or hard drives. We collectively know our faculty collective inside out. Ours is a fairly small undergraduate university, as universities go, set bang in the middle of downtown, and what with funding cuts and "what can you do with a BA?" attitude, we have not been expanding. We haven't had a new face in any department in fifteen years, except in computer-related courses, which are proliferating so fast they're going to implode even before the Y2K bug crashes all computers into a black hole.

Let us face it, we've all grown old together in this dump. The same faces, now fifteen years older: the women faculty show more wrinkles but the men are more batty. The women colour their hair, most of them, and the men don't. But then they don't grey as early, Why would they? They have no worries. They get their tenure and promotions like clockwork. They know a touch of grey makes them look distinguished. When I joined the secretarial pool, they were all in their thirties, recently out of Yale and Toronto, with their carefully unkempt hair and beard, pipes in mouth, breezily holding court in classrooms. Most of them have quit smoking. Most are clean-shaven now, just so the grey doesn't show on their chins, and some are balding, but these men always carry themselves as though they were rulers of all they survey, and women students still fall for them, though what with sexual harassment rules, times have changed. I could tell you stories of when I first came here, but of course I won't, because our middle name is confidentiality. Most now have the good sense to keep their hands off students, but not off women *per se*. As I've told you. They are in their fifties.

Between the fifteen of us, who make the old core of the secretarial staff and therefore often have lunch together in threes and fours, we've seen them all, male menopause symptoms I mean. One of the overt symptoms is cars. Alf A has bought himself a sports car, convertible of course, leather upholstery, laser CD and all. Brad B has a megahuge Roadrunner; now who would want one of those in Manipeg where the land is so flat you can see your own back, you might ask, but these monsters are in every driveway from Dallas to Bakersville and so why not in Manipeg? Chad C has bought a very expensive antique — exactly the same model as our very first car, a 1957 Chevrolet, that we drove for two years and paid someone ten dollars to tow to the auto cemetery outside the perimeter. Chad drives it during the summer, and oh the memories it brings to me of those early days when I came here a blushing bride, the henna scarce dried on my palms, and Sivaram had just bought one of those, already twelve years old but its chrome still gleamingly splashed across the side fenders ... At that time, it was a penniless student's car, but now very definitely it is connected to the m.m. syndrome.

Then there is workaholism and alcoholism, often so interconnected, one can't figure out which is cause and which effect. But we have quite a few of those as well. Edgar E has a recliner in his office because he is so hard at work, often till midnight as Tom in Security has told me, but he also has a whole bar in the filing drawer under his table; Fred F's wife, we were told, deserted him because he spent so little time at home, what with his lab and his conferences all over the world, but when we spoke about it we always said it the right way — that he deserted her long before she him. Cars, drink, overwork, all bad, and I don't want to appear like I am condoning anyone or anything, or setting up a hierarchy of greater and lesser evils.

But women, rather menopausal men's hankering after women is the worst. George G, for years one of the placid balloons around campus, shed fifty pounds and the next thing we hear it wasn't his doctor who was behind it but some young thing for whom he has left his wife of twenty some years; Henry H, it seems, met up again with his high school sweetheart at the Homecoming a couple of years ago, and now they are busy divorcing their spouses; Irving I didn't bother about divorce but just latched on to a widow ten years his senior. Yes, we have the whole gamut and these have been stories shared — confidentially, of course — at our lunches over the last few years. Everything you read in Ann Landers and then some. Yes, all this has been just in the last few years, and why? Because all these men are in their fifties. It is so clearly a menopausal thing, isn't it time we had some serious studies, for heaven's sake, that's what universities are for, to research into areas that most concern our everyday lives.

But no, scientists squint at the stars and wind tunnels and spectrometers and deal with equations yea-long about how light travels and diamonds glitter. Totally useless knowledge, when there is so much to do here, so much ego-gas right here on the ground that the place is becoming more toxic than the highly combustible air around pig farms.

If I sound really peeved at men, it is because I am, as I sit here, waiting for the clock to strike twelve, except that now my clock is digital and doesn't strike anything, and unless you are bang in front of it, it shows zeroes or ones. Did you know that seven dashes in various combinations form all the numbers from zero to twelve on the face of a digital?

The phone rings. I pick up the receiver quickly. It is not yet twelve and you know how upset callers get if secretaries aren't at their desk; not callers so much, let me be honest, but the new supervisor we have who monitors our comings and goings. Last year, there was this university-wide review of how to restructure to cut costs and what not, and the next thing we know we get Grendel's mother appointed as some kind of executive director with an office on the seventh floor, and I wouldn't be surprised if she's had camera eyes installed to beam on every secretary's chair, I swear. She phones us sweetly to ask some inanity, but we know she is spying, because it is always just before lunch or just after coffeebreak.

"Good morning, Department of English. How may I help you?"

"Hi, Maru, how you is?"

It is Chelsea, my boss Will's twelve-year-old daughter. "Hi, Chels, me is fine. How is you?" It is a ritual we have had, Chelsea and I, since she was six, which is when her mother Jan went back to nursing, which meant shift work, and Will had to take on various chauffeuring duties. In the last few years, she had spent a lot of time here, swinging quietly in her dad's office chair while he was at meetings. But now she was in grade seven, and I seldom saw her. Her older siblings I had never known that well, but I was Chelsea's pal.

"Could I speak to Dad, please?"

"He is busy, Chels sweetie, can I take a message?"

"I have to remind him about my special piano class, please."

"I'll do it for you, Chels, I hear you are going for gold, eh?" She had won the school contest and was now going for the provincial, which was the reason for the extra classes.

"So, why can't I speak to him, you Cerberus guarding the gates?"

"You've been reading the mythology book I gave you for your birthday!"

"Only just enough to impress you, Maru, you are so gullible. So, beam me up to Dad."

"I told you, Chels, he is busy right now. Want to call him back in ten minutes?"

"Don't think so, but don't forget, thanks. 'Bye."

I recorded a message on Will's phone before replacing the receiver. I didn't want to call him. The Woman was with him.

The Woman. Now you know what all this is about. Yes, my boss Will is having an affair, because he is fifty-four and is in that awful phase of life. Suffice it to say she is from up there, the Administration on the seventh floor. She is one of those slim, shapely women with alabaster skin and padded breasts, or implants maybe, who always wear three hundred dollar outfits and heels. I've never seen Will in a tie or jacket, and I'd have thought from the papers I type for him to send to literary journals that he'd go for a full-blooded feminist in jeans and Birkenstocks, but here was the stereotypical other woman of executive soap operas.

You'll say I am jealous. I am not above jealousy. I admit I go to Siv's lab once in a while to keep tab on his assistants. Once, in one of my lows, I went there looking for the other woman: every secretary was trim and smart, and every research assistant super-intelligent and youthful, but none was his kind, I decided. But then I went home, and I knew it could have been any of those women. Turned out that wasn't the problem at all, but that is another story, and you can read it some day in "Maru and the Volvo."

But this is Erika Jonsson I am dealing with now. And I am not jealous of her. Just a tad sick. Some others are jealous of her. She came in from the blue, and did not rise from the ranks to the seventh floor as so many others did. She came in from the mega Great-West Life across downtown, from one ivory tower to another, and we have watched her antics the five years she's been here, what with so many menopausal men who come for meetings or work on the seventh floor. By the time one gets to the seventh floor, one is usually in the m.m. phase of life, as you should know, except that Erika got there early because of all the hype about affirmative action for women. I had always been on her side at all our lunch-talks, admired her for her elegance, her level-headed taking charge of administrative decisions on committees where I'd worked with her. I had even sided with her when she changed her name from Erica Johnson to Erika Jonsson, thumbs up for heritage cultures and all that. But this was too close to home. Will, our easy-going, anecdote-loving Will, whose table was always a vortex of chaos, whose guffaws rang up and down the hallways as he chatted with colleagues, what could he possibly see in this caryatid of proficiency?

No, I take that back. Of course, any man would be attracted to Erika, especially someone like Will. She had all that Will lacked — organizational skills and elegance. And, of course, sexuality. Fit the m.m. syndrome to a T. But the problem was that this was too close to home. I knew not only Will's wife but Erika's husband, Jim. They lived on the next street: he was a good guy, one of those pillars-of-community-life people who would volunteer for all community club events and coach kids' hockey teams and come over with shovel and sand if he saw you stuck in your driveway some winter morning. How could she do this to Jim? And they had kids still at school. He probably didn't have a clue about what was going on at the University. He was a manager at one of the department stores, fairly high up on the totem pole. But these two orbits don't intersect — the university here and life out there in the working world. Unless there were happenstance crossovers ... like me and Erika.

Just in case Will didn't take his phone messages, I scribbled a note about Chelsea's piano lesson and placed it in his mailbox. I could hear Erika's laugh from his room. She has a pleasant laugh. The main problem is that I want to dislike her but can't. I've known her for years as a good neighbour, and it is really difficult to brush away what is happening the way I can brush away all the other affairs that we talk about at lunchtime and store impersonally in our heads.

Too close to home; I keep saying that and it should be clear to you by now as to where I am going with this. Sivaraman is fifty-four, that awfully vulnerable age when men seem to go batty. And he is still handsome as Adonis, his Adam's apple as sexy as ever, and his grey-tinged hair above his flat forehead is charismatic no matter from what angle you see him. He is in Ottawa on a special two-year stint at the National Research Council, and now I am in a flap what with all these affairs going on around me.

We have a house in Rockcliffe — that's Siv, nothing but top drawer for him — and I am here in Manipeg. No can do. We had a rough time ten years ago, as I said, but I was thirty-six at the time, and there is a big diff between thirty-six and forty-six in a woman's life. Take it from me, there is.

So I decided I'd resign and join him long-term, instead of these weekend hops we've been having for the last year. Mind you, this last year has been rather great; when he comes over, we have a quiet time, and I actually cook a decent meal every day, and we watch some old movies or listen to one of the new CDs of some old opera. When I go over to the nation's capital it is party time, mostly hosted by us, to pay back some of the parties he was invited to in my absence, and I love parties. Especially Ottawa parties where you never meet the same people twice, unlike here where we have the same set of some forty couples playing musical chairs — if we don't run into them at one party, for sure they'll be at the next.

Yes, it's been a good life, except for this epidemic of m.m. that is sweeping through my world. And which has made me resign my niche at the university and head out for the hill.

While I waited for Maureen and Jane, who were to pick me up on the way to the Dining Room, there were two students who came in for help. One wanting to know when Bob will be back and the other to pick up her paper.

At lunch, Jane had yet another tidbit to add. Joe J in her department got thrown out of his house last Saturday by his irate wife who had received an anonymous phone call about his current affair. For twenty years, she had put up with his womanizing, and she'd at last got what it takes to throw him and his briefcase out. We all knew she had known all along, but often it takes that push to do what is needed. That a third person should actually talk about it did it for her. The force be with her, we said, and drank to it. It being my last day and all, we decided a glass of wine was in order.

Jane said she'd have to leave early because her Eliot paper was soon due and she had to go to the library before getting back to her desk. That led me to expound to the others my reading of T.S. Eliot's "The Love Song of J. Alfred Prufrock." It was so clearly a case study of male menopause, I said, and explained all about his fear of going bald, getting insomnia and how terrified he was about not being able to perform. "That's neat," she said, once she understood that the reference to a peach was not just about his teeth, "How come you know Eliot? I mean, why would anyone want to read Eliot unless they had to?" I told her I had taken a few English courses the time I was with the Psych Department, just as I had taken Psych and Anthro and Geog courses during my stint at the English Department.

There was no point telling her about the Seventies, when I had come with hopes I could complete the Master's in English in which I had been enrolled when I was whisked off-campus, wedded, bedded and sent off to keep house halfway around the world for that starved looking young man with an Adam's apple that was so sexy. When I tried to enrol for a Master's here, I was told that anyone who has a BA from India would be given only the equivalent of a high school diploma. I would have to start all over again. And I did: but then the boys started coming, first Arvind, then Nari. Then I started working part time, and by the time Giri started school, the rules had changed and my Indian BA was recognized. But by then it was too late for me. I just continued to take courses for the fun of it, because employees are given flex time to enrol in courses. It was fun, to take course after freshman course.

"That's neat, Maru, I think I'll steal that reading for my term paper."

"Not a good idea, " I said. "I got it from the same person with whom you are taking the course."

"I'll be darned, I didn't know Una had been here that long, since your time."

"That long, thanks," I said, sounding peeved. But then I laughed because Jane often doesn't hear my jokes; it happens often enough; just because I look different and have a bit of an accent, people think I can't joke. "No, she wasn't here when I took my freshman course, but I know just when she formulated that reading. It was during one of those big departmental flaps some years ago when everyone was breathing fire and firing off memos — all of which I had to type, mind you. So I don't think it will go well with her to have her own idea placed on her plate."

Maureen said, "I don't know about that; could happen she'll be so pleased she'll give you an A. Imitation is the best form of flattery, you know. By the way, I read somewhere that the term is andropause."

Jane said, "Why not stick to plain old 'midlife crisis'"

I said, "I like MMS, parallel to PMS. Don't you think it has the right sound?"

This news about Joe J kept us longer than our usual hour, and I rushed down, back to my desk. If we aren't at our desk by one o'clock, there's always flak and griping from one or other of the scores of people we seemed to be accountable to. As I've said already: What was I doing here, I asked myself, good riddance to this straitjacket job and this m.m. environment. Ottawa, here I come.

*****

On Saturday, I had some work at the downtown Bay, and so parked my car at the U. and did my shopping. When I came back, I remembered I had to go up to the library. I had unearthed two borrowed books when packing for Ottawa last night. The fines are horrendous and the

Desk doesn't spare anyone these days. You cough up the fine or else. I went up to the library to return the books, and instead of just throwing them into the book bin, I went through the doors to say hello to Connie who was at the circulation desk. After a short chat, I went up to my favourite spot in the topmost level of the library. It would be the twelfth floor if we numbered them along with the rest of the building, but it is merely called Level 5. It is a large study space with windows on all four sides, lined with cubicles. On the way to my favourite cubicle, where I sometimes spent my afternoon coffee breaks, I paused at the side that overlooked the south. There was the Curling Club, stashed away behind Safeway, and I remembered how we had got roped into a curling team the very first winter we were here, and me flying like a witch with the broom tucked between my legs and being really glad when I did come to a stop that Newton's first law of motion was a myth after all.

My favourite cubicle is by one of the many large windows that overlook the west, with the Arena in the distance and the hospital closer by. I remembered Giri's birth, weeks before he was due, and me lying at the Women's Pavilion, that was what it was called in those days, thinking of him all tubed up in the intensive-care unit where, they told me, he was doing very well, but of course I didn't believe them. After a whole day of postnatal blues and the most excruciating pain, I got up from bed, intent on walking down to the nursery, wherever it was, and seeing my baby. I looked out the window: across a field of snow was the familiar tower of the Admin. Wing. My university. I knew then that Giri was fine, that the sky was blue, that God was in his heaven and all was right with the world. My husband, my new baby, my university, what else could anyone ask for?

Now, as I stood at the window, looking at the green pipes of the hospital, I felt deep nostalgia for the place, my place. What the hell was I doing leaving all this for Ottawa, that city of bureaucrats and bullshit? What would I do there? Sure I enjoyed all those parties and socializing that I was immersed in on every weekend trip I took but, I mean, what would I *really* do?

I went down the escalator, feeling quite blue. I couldn't help walking past the escalator down the familiar hallway to my office. I needed to sit quietly for a while, a last private good bye to my niche. I still had my key. I opened the door and closed it behind me.

Oh, how I was going to miss my office, not mine any more, I told myself, as I sat on my chair, not mine even though the next occupant wasn't likely to come for a couple of weeks.

God, I'll miss this, I said to myself, looking at the bus depot that had spewed toxins for years, and was no doubt the cause of the cancers that had been picking off so many of our members: yes, but I'd still miss it.

When I first joined the staff, I was in another department but all offices were the same, they always are. We had electric typewriters, and I had to retype the whole page every time: there was so much typing to be done, for of course, the faculty didn't type. Then came the memory-line typewriters where we could proofread and correct a line at a time before going on to the next. Then came computers. One would have thought life for us would have become easier now that most faculty did their own typing at their own computers, but no, we seem to be just as busy every minute of every day as we were back then. At first, the Chair of the Department and I were the only ones who had a phone, and I had to take messages for all of the faculty, including from wives who wanted bread or milk picked up by the men on their way home. In those days, faculty had to take a key from me to open a little phone room end of the hallway. We used to laugh about it at lunch, how we felt like a primary school teacher, or a gas station attendant, handing them a key to a little room. But now, everyone has their own phone and answering machine to boot, and only little Chelsea phones me asking for her dad.

At this thought, all my grief and anger surfaced again: these men, who couldn't figure out right from wrong or what was good for them from what was bad, these menopausal men for whom one couldn't work any more.

There was a knock from the inside door, and I jolted into position. Will poked his head in and said, "Hello, Maru, what are you doing here? I thought you had put every last bit of paper in order already."

I didn't ask him what he was doing here. Probably waiting for his lady love. Worse, she must be in there. Ugh. I'd better not be in his way.

"Just leaving," I said. "You go right ahead with whatever you were doing."

"Do you have a minute, Maru?"

"Sure." I put my bag back on the floor.

"I hope you enjoy yourself in Ottawa, but I'll miss you."

"Thanks, I'm sure my replacement will do a dandy job."

He must have registered my distance. I didn't have to hide it any more.

"I have to know this, Maru, just off the record, I know it makes sense for you to be with Siv. But why now? I mean why not last year, when he moved? Another ten months and he will be back."

I didn't answer. I just shrugged.

"I've got to know, Maru, is it because I am being an egregious ass?"

My old friendliness almost came back. How could you be angry with someone who knew he was being an egregious ass?

"I'd be lying if I said it isn't part of the reason," I said. "Others' private lives are none of my business and all that, Will, but yes, I do find it difficult, knowing everyone involved and all that."

"The heart has its reasons."

"Exactly, Will, my heart too has its reasons."

"I do admire your sense of loyalty."

I shrugged. He thought I was talking about Jim and Jan but his comment was apropos.

"Listen, Maru, you don't have to resign, you know, you can just get a transfer to another department. I mean, I feel I like I am responsible for you giving up a perfectly good job that you've always enjoyed."

"Don't worry, Will. It's my decision, and not your responsibility at all."

"I do worry, what will you do out there, Maru?"

"Write my memoirs? You know I've always wanted to write my magnum opus, "Maru and the Maple Leaf" ..."

"How you came here a blushing bride with the henna scarce dried on your palm?"

I laughed more easily now. I loved that sentence of mine, and everyone, these guys and the other seccys., threw it my way whenever they could.

"Look, Maru, why don't you get this writing bug out of your system. Sign-up for the Three-Day Novel Contest this year and get it out of your system so you can settle back full time where you belong — on that chair."

He seemed so genuinely concerned that I almost told him the real reason why I was leaving — that the male menopausal rampage around me had driven me to fear for myself and for poor Siv who was at that vulnerable age of fifty-four.

But I didn't say anything, having heard the patronizing undercurrent that he wasn't even aware of in himself. As though I belonged to that chair, poor man, what would an English prof at a backwater university know about who I really was? About my family back in India, or even that Siv is one of the top brass in the scientific scene in Canada, or about the VIP social schedule I had in Ottawa, or about my three marvellous sons, whom I had nurtured. Or about all my work in the ethnic and art and women's communities over the years.

If I ever had to go to a shrink, I guess she'd figure out that I've never reconciled myself to being a secretary; everyone in my family who went out into the working world, and my family is spread all over the globe, is a professor or executive. Had I married someone who lived in India, I'd have completed my Master's and joined the faculty, and then I'd have completed my PhD and become a professor by now; instead of which I am here, on this secretary's chair. The shrink might come to the conclusion that I resented all this, but let us face it, life is a package deal — you can't choose just parts, or put another way, you had to choose between PC and Macintosh, and I had chosen Mac because Siv was the Mac harddrive. Some of the software is interchangeable but the harddrive is the heart. And the secretary's chair is what came with it.

True, my derriere has expanded over the years sitting on this chair, but that is just a little part of me, as are all the other parts of wife, mother, social worker. Me, the real holistic me, only I knew, and Siv maybe, if he hadn't forgotten now in the throes of m.m.

"Maybe I'll come back when Siv returns to his job here."

"Good, good, that's only another ten months, right? So just take leave without pay, and rewrite your resignation. You have time till your vacation period ends. Please do that, Maru, what with all your union rules, you'd better take care of it first thing Monday morning, right?"

"I'll think about it, Will. Have a good weekend."

"You too." He smiled, and I could feel myself softening. But he was fifty-four and behaving batty. I could not work for him. Even aside from the fear that my own nest was on fire.

Two

Siv met me at the airport. He gave me a bear hug and seemed genuinely glad to see me. "What a relief to have you here at last, Maroo," he said. But wasn't he being too effusive? Never trust anyone who is too effusive. I suddenly remembered one of my English profs back in India. Having just returned from the United States — in those days, many profs went for a couple of years to the States and came back with a PhD — he of course had to broadcast it in all the usual ways — not wearing a tie and jacket but a loose Hawaiian shirt that was popular in these parts those days, not giving lectures but making students give seminar papers (and thereby sparing himself all work, it seemed to us), telling us all kinds of personal anecdotes while dropping names left, right and centre — William Riley Parker, the Milton biographer, the guy who wrote the first documentation manual for English studies, Cleanth Brooks, Robert Penn Warren, Saul Bellow. He would drop these names as though he met them at the pub every evening. We were tired of his "When I was in America" bragging, but couldn't do anything about it. This professor had a very young wife — she seemed twenty years his junior, I swear — and he was forever bringing her to the Department — another unheard of thing — and forever putting his arms around her, which made us girls blush no end and gave the male students ideas ... To make a long story short, he suddenly found himself a guru, so he said, some recluse who lived in a cave forty miles from the city, and who had taken a vow of silence. And our prof would go every weekend with his tape recorder — it was a huge, clunky reel-to-reel, this was the early Seventies, remember — and presumably recorded his guru's silence. He vanished one day, leaving his young wife and two children, and the next thing we heard, he had an ashram in California, gave lectures about the inner self, and published expensive glossy books which had photographs of rows of beautiful blondes in saffron robes sitting cross-legged in the lotus pose of meditation. Never trust a man who is over-emotive.

Usually, I am the one who keeps the conversation going, but I kept quiet, to test what Siv would do. He seemed quite at ease: he didn't even switch on the radio; he talked instead, of all the people in his project, and how it had to pick up pace in the next six months. Oh, by the way, he said, I've booked a table at the Olive Garden for us and Ramesh Ukkal — he's writing a biography of Professor. Hope you don't mind me fixing it up without checking with you. He is leaving for Stanford tomorrow, and I want to know where he is going with the usual stories.

Siv was worried about any biography anyone might be writing or thinking of writing about Professor. He was rather possessive of

Professor, as was each of the hundred students who had worked with him.

Professor Ramaswami was Sivaram's mentor, a gigantic icon on India's science screen, a living legend while he lived. His students called him Professor, no first or last name, just Professor, and he was the only one they called so, which is why I call them only profs., if you've noticed. He was also my uncle, and I had spent many summers in his house, because his wife Chittammai had no daughters of her own, and so borrowed me or one of my girl cousins from time to time. As a child, I thought of him as a holy terror; one recurring incident I cannot forget was his sudden bloodcurdling shouting at night for the watchman, an old man deaf as a doornail to the rest of the world but always alert to his master's voice. The old man would come running, his stick going clackety clack, and Professor would tell him to stop the dog from barking or the tom cat from mewing or some other sound that only he could hear, and the watchman would say "Ji hazur," and obediently trot off to the gate to yell at the watchman of the house from where the bark or mew just might have come. I have so many wonderful memories of this mad scientist, but once married to Siv, I had to curb my raconteuring about his insanities. He was not an uncle any more, but Professor. So quickly had Siv brainwashed me that when I first came to this country and went to one of those drive-in theatres and saw giant figures on the superlarge screen something in me resisted that sacrilege: how could anyone except Professor ever be allowed to be so huge?

As soon as we reached home, Siv checked his voice mail. That's him: he does it even when he comes home straight from his lab, as though some earthshaking news could have happened in the fifteen minutes it takes from lab to home. There was a message on the answering machine that the 3:30 meeting would be in Room 440 instead of Room 224.

He took off after a cup of coffee.

I sat over my coffee for a few minutes, briefly wondering whether the phone call was a preplanned one. But now that I was actually here, everything seemed normal: of course Siv wasn't having an affair. It is always like that. Things are always blown way of out of proportion by one's imagination: like hearing all those awful things about life in downtown Chicago or New York and once there, feeling they are as safe as any other city; or my phobia about flying — every time I book a flight, I am sure it was going to be my last, that the plane would crash a fiery hell, but once on the plane, there's something about it that makes one feel it is safe as houses, and I don't even bother to listen to the usual safety instructions about oxygen masks and flotation devices.

Wait, I am being illogical here. Just because people who live in downtown Chicago or New York think they won't get mugged doesn't mean they won't. Same way, small town people might blow the fear out of proportion but the fear is not out of line. Oh, why do men have to turn fifty-four?

After coffee, I moved to the living room for a while. It was always a pleasure to see the sweeping curve of the staircase, the oak bannisters that had aged into a mellow texture where the solid oak grains were elitistically discreet unlike contemporary woodwork where the lines came right out of the kitchen cabinets and slapped you. It was a beautiful house: its owner, Stephen Wilde, was the head of one of the departments at the National Research Council, and had gone away to Brazil for two years, on a project of course, even though everyone knew it was because he had to get away after his ex-wife's book came out last year, one of those socialite autobiographies where the author paints a lurid picture of spousal abuse and ends up finding true love and life in a woman's arms. The Wildes are an old Rockcliffe family, as anyone who is anyone in Ottawa should know, and Stephen is just one of the twelve or so Wildes who live on this hill. But like so many old families that inflation had deflated, he had not remodelled the house in decades and the fuel bills were astronomical: we didn't know that of course when we rented it, and the rent had sounded extremely reasonable, for Rockcliffe that is. It is one of the smallest houses there, and does not have a river view or anything, but it does have solid oak staircases and curved walls.

I went upstairs. As usual, Siv had not opened the curtains, probably not since my last visit. I drew them open and the afternoon sunlight flooded in. Our bedroom overlooked the backyard of a manor house, owned by the CEO of a mega multinational corporation, and their swimming pool is the size of Lake Huron. Even though it was a good distance away, we could see a lot of flesh in the summer months: at first, I had sat with binoculars and watched through Venetian blinds to the cavorting of the rich and famous, but flesh is flesh, and there is only so much one needs. Except readers of tabloids, who seem to need them the way vampires need human blood.

There was something different about the bedroom. Ah yes, it was the hologram. It was missing. The wall was a blank. What could have happened to it? I looked in the closets first, thinking it had fallen and Siv had stashed away the pieces, meaning to clean them up, of course, but never getting around to it. Then I went into the other rooms. It was in Siv's den, propped up against a bookshelf on one of the rubberneck stools I had in the closet of every room to reach up to the top shelves of bookshelves and closets. It wasn't broken or anything. Siv had even placed a doily on the stool under it. I looked closely. There were a couple of dry flower petals on the doily. Whoa, what was the matter?

I knew Siv loved that picture. He had it even before I came into his life. In Manipeg, he had it at his lab office. I liked it too because it was first of that kind I had seen, and this was before the high-tech holograms of today. It was a night sky, with faint stars and constellations: there were two beams of light, one from each lower corner shooting diagonally upwards, like from two flashlights — from one angle you could see just one of the beams, from another the other, but if you moved your eyes just right, the two beams intersected, collided, merged, and there was a meteor fall of colours, resplendent, like neverending Deepavali firecrackers. The Crossing of the Lights, Siv explained, that is what the Brahmin ritual of *sandhyavandanam* was — the recognition that when the lights crossed the sky at dawn, noon and dusk, something happened, some magical effluence; and that is why the learned ones faithfully saluted the crossing of lights with the sacred syllables of the Gayatri mantra.

I never thought I'd marry someone who did his sandhya every day. I assumed when my marriage was arranged with this young man from North America that he would be like one of my brothers or cousins, cavalier about customs. The first thing that struck me on our honeymoon in Ooty when I woke up with a start to hear the water running and the clock hands on five-fifteen was, *Oh no, if marriages are made in heaven, why doesn't someone up there not think about simple compatibility and match larks to larks, owls to owls? I have always been an owl, most comfortable going to bed late and getting up late, and here I was married to someone who started the day at five-fifteen, for heavens' sake!* Then I heard him showering. I assumed it was because of the steamy lovemaking of the honeymoon, and went back to sleep; but the next morning, after his shower, I heard him at his sandhya. That threw me for a loop. I come from a family of lukewarm-at-best believers; of course, my brothers had all gone through the sacred-thread ceremony at the age of thirteen or fourteen, and had groaningly awoken and muttered their way through the sandhya for a month after the ceremony, after which the family priest stopped coming and they stopped the ritual. One of my cousins, who had never been given his sacred thread because his dad had been with the World Bank in

Switzerland during his teens and had forgotten all about it, had to have it hush-hush on the eve of his wedding, for of course one had to be initiated into that phase of learning the scriptures before one was allowed to enter the householder's state of matrimony. The family priest was most upset, but he upheld his loyalty to the family honour by not saying a word to anyone about the last minute ritual.

That was the extent of the sandhya in my family. But here was this young man fresh come from America, who still went through the daily rites. It blew me away.

But soon, what with his PhD thesis unravelling, Arvind turning up, and then Nari and Giri, the morning rites went out the window. After all these years, had he taken it up again? Whoa.

I asked him that at dinner time. Not quite, he said, but he was chanting the Gayatri. He wanted to chant a hundred thousand Gayatris.

I asked him why he would want such meaningless repetition. A hundred thousand would take forever, I said.

"No, Maroo," he said, "you really should try to include 'finite' in your vocabulary. At one minute per Gayatri, it would take one hundred thousand minutes which is one thousand six hundred and sixty-seven hours which is just under sixty weeks, if one could spare four hours a day. As a matter of fact, twenty-four syllables shouldn't take more than thirty seconds. So one could cut that time in half."

"But why?"

"An experiment," he said. "At the end of one hundred thousand Gayatris, it is said that something would happen, an effluence, a spiritual tejas, a power."

"Grandma used to write one hundred and eight Sri Rama Jayams every morning," I said. "She said one crore of them would give her moksha."

"Still a finite number but at one hundred and eight a day, ten million lines would take approximately two hundred and fifty years. If she'd stepped it up to a thousand a day, maybe ..."

"Poor grandma, she should have had a calculator."

"She probably did, in her head. But she also probably believed she could start her next life with the bank deposit still in her name and go on from where she left off at this life."

"You don't have to laugh at her."

"Does it seem like I am?"

"You mean it? About your one hundred thousand Gayatris?"

"Of course."

"You are a scientist," I said.

"Look who's laughing at whom," he said.

"You are a scientist," I repeated, more exasperated.

"Precisely," he said, "that is why I have to prove or disprove it by experiment and not by just pooh-poohing it or promulgating it as truth. We know for sure that there are force fields around transformers that adversely influence brain development: maybe the ancients knew how to transform force fields into positive energy."

"You don't really believe it, do you?"

"No I don't, one Immanuel Velikovsky per century is enough."

"Isn't he the one who wrote *The Golden Bough* of science? Taking all kinds of parallels from different cultures and saying the Flood was a real occurrence that different cultures recorded in different ways?"

"Exactly."

"I rather like that idea. What's wrong with that?"

"He can be given A+ for imagination and zilch for methodology. His data-collection was faulty, his translations were faulty, he himself was a good example of collective amnesia — he displaced into his subconscious the awful truth that theory has to be backed by experimental data."

"So you are spoofing him."

"Yes. I am. But — always the big Ifs and Buts. But, on the other hand, one shouldn't dismiss something out of hand: Wegener's continental drift concept and Chandrasekhar's black hole theory were driven into cold storage for forty years, but are now accepted as canonical."

"So you think something will happen at the end of one lakh Gayatris? If so, how come no one has done it yet? Should be easy enough to do by those sadhus who sit in caves and do diddly yet have food brought to them by suckers. They can say it for ten hours a day, surely? Lots of people could have done it."

"How do we know they didn't? Once one sees the light, one usually decides to leave society, so naturally we don't hear of them."

"No one just leaves. There is always the urge to tell someone, anyone."

"In most things, yes, but this kind of spiritual experience might be in a different league. Hinduism never did go for proselytisation."

"So you believe in this Gayatri thing?"

"No, and that is why I should be the one to do the experiment, don't you agree? I wish I could spare four hours but two is all I've managed most days.

I gave up. It made no sense. I had a sneaking suspicion he actually believed in this mumbo jumbo. A senior scientist at the National Research Council. Maybe, I realized with alarm, this is m.m.! Well, better crazy science than shapely blondes. Except, of course, it could be both.

Three

For the first little while, life was the way it had been with any of my other short visits — a flurry of parties that we had to host to repay for all those that Siv had gone to in my absence. Then, the pace slowed down. It started sinking in that I was here to stay. Siv had brought home one of his old computers for me even before I came, and he now started nagging me to do something worthwhile, like writing all those stories from the time "I came here a blushing bride, the henna scarce dried on my palms."

One day I did start on this long-dreamt of project. Once at the computer, my writing really took off. It was like one of those three-day novel contests where you shut yourself in a room, and zoom, take off into the wild blue yonder.

My writing was going really well. I had found my voice. Voice, ah, that magic word that my Creative Writing instructors talked about — yes, I took several of those courses, too, over the years.

I wrote about my community work experiences — the time Folklorama first started and my work for the India Pavilion, the time I started all those dance courses in the late Seventies, the time I had a weekly television show "helping Indo-Canadians stand tall" sort of thing, and then the heady days of my work with the Immigrant Women's Association which took me to Ottawa and all that, and then, wow, the headiest perhaps of them all in that it gave me the most humungous headache ever — the time I was Chair of a local literary guild. I wrote all these and more, with just the right mix of spoof and social commentary. Then came December, and that month has a way of cutting into everything else.

Pre-empting everything, every single thing, including my voice. Gone, all gone. I never thought I'd lose my voice. I had only dreaded that the computer, old that it was, would conk out. I could imagine that if it got annoyed with me, like Chanakya of old, it would eat up my files, and spit out the seeds. I made copies of every file on different floppies and then of course I couldn't figure out which was the latest version. I should know better, having been a secretary for fifteen years, that I should file and label everything here just as I did at my office desk in Manipeg. Should have stuck to habits. Old habits die hard but older habits die harder. Deep within, I am an academic, like everyone else in my family for the last three generations. I have never seen a clean study table in my growing years. It just wasn't done. There was an implicitly assumed connection between clean tables and cleaned-out brains, and that people had to have messy tables if they laid any claims to intelligence.

When I was on the Board of the Immigrant Women's Association, I got involved in setting up the Counselling Section. That was when I came to know about life as really lived: all the beating and battering that women endured. Now, of course, new laws and the media have helped educate everyone, and you can't open a newspaper without all the lurid details of spousal abuse: this morning's paper had a story about three generations of women of the same family who put up with shit because that is what they had grown up with — every woman in the family had been battered by her spouse. I know I am trying to excuse my sloppiness at home by drawing on non-equivalent examples. But still and all, maybe we are what we grow up with. That is why I don't get as impatient as some women I work with when I hear some man saying only alcoholics are violent or some harebrained report says there is no spousal abuse or child molestation in this ethnic community or that. Some lucky ones, like me, really didn't experience this in their growing years and many others didn't know about it because women have always kept it hidden from kids. We had a servant maid who from time to time came with swollen arms and face, but she always described her fall or stove accident or whatever reason she had cooked up in such detail, that I and her children believed her, not knowing any better.

So where was I? Oh yes, about me starting on my magnum opus and not getting anywhere. Do you see the pattern of my life? Something always comes up to impede my moving towards what I was born to be. A writer, that is what I was born to be. But Christmas stopped my flow.

Then something else came up that promised to get me back on track, something I never believed could happen. Chikkamma came back into my life.

It was that time between Christmas and New Year. You know what a twilight zone it can be sometimes, that week, maybe that is why everyone runs around malls, to get away from that grey zone which can really get to you if you sit still. I reluctantly sat up and fluffed the cushions on the couch where I had been having a catnap. I had to run down to the corner store for some bread and milk. The room echoed with sounds of Christmas, carols sung at the Club party two days before Christmas, glasses clinking with Christmas toasts, and the laughter of voices as family and friends had filled in the year's news to each other.

But behind these recent echoes I heard the murmur of women's voices, a soothing sound that had become part of my life of late, of women sitting around a white dhoti or sari or bedsheet spread on the ground, flattening warm balls of sago paste or squeezing rice-flour dough through the press to make *vadams* that would be dried in the terrace sun, and deep fried for festive meals, or on monsoon days when vegetables were not plenteous. The voices rose and fell, with little laughs or sighs as the story demanded, as they shared them old and new, of a grandchild's first words or a daughter's still birth, of bargains over stainless steel pots and pans in exchange for gold-thread of old saris, of what they did or planned to do with the monthly draw money that almost every one put in one pool or other, money that came in a lump sum at Deepavali time if you were lucky. Some days there were more sighs than laughs, when someone reported she had seen so and so with eyes or arms that bore evidence of more than love-bites. But details were never mentioned, blame never assigned, the menfolk never chastised. Ah, it was a hard life for some women, alas to be a born a woman.

The voices rose and fell in soft murmurs, while sheet after sheet filled with flattened dough took its place on the terrace, each covered with a top sheet that was kept from blowing away with stones placed at each corner. Some times children of the hostess or one of the other women, came to them, and were given a small ball or two of the gooey paste — no, not one little bit more, you will get a stomach ache if you eat it raw — and then shooed away. This was woman's work, and had to be done in time, while the sun beat down on the cement terraces.

I found myself listening to the soothing murmur for a few minutes longer each time nowadays before getting back to my chores.

Snow fell softly on the lawn outside.

I heard the letter carrier at the door, or so I thought. When I opened the door, I let out a squeal at a small, lithe figure who entered. "Chikkamma! What a surprise! Come in, come in." I opened my arms but then shied away as my visitor raised her right hand in admonishment. "How is one supposed to greet you, Chikkamma, maybe I should fall on my knees and touch your feet ...? But you were never one for tradition, were you? This is such a surprise! I have thought of you so often over the years, and now to see you face to face, I never imagined ..."

"I see you are stumped for words. Not a good omen, one might say, to be losing your vocabulary. Writing your memoirs, I hear, but only about your life since you came here, from what I can see. For twenty years we feed you and teach you and tend you through mumps and measles and diarrhoea and whatnot, and bang-slam, you shut the door and write only about curling and Manipeg and your feminist friends."

"I mean, it isn't like that. I do plan to write about my whole life, honest, not just about Canada."

"I'll believe it when I see it," she snorted, seating herself on the rocker as though she had been there all her life.

"How did you know I was writing? Oh, it must be Aunt Meena: I did show her some of it when she stopped in from Frisco after visiting her son."

Chikkamma placed her large cloth bag next to her chair and gestured she wanted it to stay right there.

"Of course, of course, no problem," I hastened to my hosting duties. "Can I get you some coffee? Maybe tea would be good?"

"What I would really like is some hot chukku vellam to clear my throat, but I don't expect you'd have any. So, no thanks, I am fine. Sit down, Maru, don't pace in circles like a cat that has just littered."

I sat on the couch, next to the rocker. It was incredible. Chikkamma had not changed one wee bit. She sat ramrod straight as always, stretching her five foot one frame to an intimidating height; her grey hair was curly and tightly knotted into a little bun at the back, and she wore the generic Conjeevaram silk sari that she had always worn, very small checks of white and some nondescript colour that changed with each sari. She must have owned a dozen of these checkered saris but I had always thought of them as one generic sari. And she was here! Chikkamma was here, in my living room in Ottawa this December afternoon. Incredible.

"Your annual Christmas letter, that cyclostyled form letter that you send to everyone ..."

"Xeroxed, yes, but not a form letter, no, Chikkamma, you can't call it a form letter," I interrupted, touched to the quick that the long letter I laboured over so lovingly every year and mailed to a large circle of family and friends in India and elsewhere, with small changes that personalized some letters thanks to the computer, was dismissed as a form letter.

Chikkamma held up her hand admonishingly. Or maybe it wasn't held up admonishingly, but having grown up under that gesture from mother, aunts and grandmother, I felt chided. I ran my hand over my own greying hair to remind myself that I was my own woman, not an awkward child in front of a reprimanding adult.

Chikkamma continued as though I had not spoken. "Your annual letter arrived just as I was leaving for here, and so I know all about what everyone in your family has done this past year. So let's not waste time over formalities. Coming straight to the point, it was news of your daughter-in-law's pregnancy that sent you scurrying to your typewriter, right?"

I gasped. I had not made the connection, but yes, Arvind and Kathy had come the Labour Day weekend, and, yes, Kathy was just beginning to show, rather early yes, she was hardly three months gone, and yes, she did look so beautiful, fragile and hardy at the same time, and yes, I had started my memoirs the day they left. The dishwasher had not been cleared of the previous day's dinner plates e*t cetera* so I had stacked the lunch things on the counter, wiped the table clean (an old habit from the old country — if you want, and want to show that you want, the guests to visit again you should clear their plates from the table and wipe it clean before they leave, a sign that they are always welcome to another meal there, and may it be in the near future). I did something quite uncharacteristic of me — I had taken out my kumkum box and placed a red dot on Kathy — a long and happy married life blessed with children — before hugging them goodbye. Then I had gone to the computer and had typed the title — "Maru and the Maple Leaf". I couldn't remember if I had typed much else, but Chikkamma was right — I had started my memoirs the day Kathy, her figure just beginning to curve with pregnancy, had left with her husband, my son Arvind.

"You are probably right, Chikkamma. I doubt I will have as much to show for it at the end of nine months, but I guess there is something about a pregnant body that sends writers on the birthing path."

Chikkamma laughed, a small snorty kind of laugh that reminded me of my other favourite aunt, Chittammai of biting tongue and colourful adages. Chittammai would never miss a chance for a nastily pertinent retort, like "Yes, especially menopausal women."

But Chikkamma was not given to such hard-hitting retorts. She said, "Don't worry. Gandhari carried for two years."

"Oh, no! Don't talk of her! Considering what she came up with at the end of it!"

"Sh, don't say inauspicious things. Everything will go well if you would just write about the right thing, instead of getting stuck in elevators."

How did she know that? How could she ever know that I had written about getting stuck in the elevator in one of my Immigrant Women's Association stories. How? I had very definitely edited it out as slowing the pace, so how could she have known?

"And not the first time either. How many stories have you started on in your life and left halfway? At least Gandhari delivered her fetus, even if she did hack it into a hundred pieces. And Duryodhan was not all that bad as he is made out to be, you know. You really should write about him, the way you wrote about Karna."

I brightened, flattered that Chikkamma should refer to one my first stories. "You're abso right, Chikkamma, I've always wanted to know more about Duryodhan. I think he was rather noble, fighting great odds, you know, the way everyone was always praising his cousins endlessly. Yes, considering the cards he drew, I think he played really well."

Chikkamma smiled.

I continued, "I am so happy to see you, after all these years of me thinking and thinking about you, Chikkamma, this is just so incredible!!!!!!"

"Ramrama, don't go on and on. For everything there's a selfish motive. I have come to stake my claim, what else? If you are really going to start writing, well, you have to write my story, and don't you forget that."

"But of course you know why I haven't been able to. You've been buzzing around in my head for years but how can I write when you haven't told me anything."

"Oh come, Maru, excuses, excuses."

"One teeny weeny bit of info is all I have."

"Isn't that enough?"

"How can it be? I can't even to begin to understand why you did such a thing."

"There are enough people still around who remember me. That is what biographers are supposed to do. Dig around, ask people."

"But why have you never told me anything? Why can't you be like Chittammai? Now she was such a wonderful storyteller, and she's given me so much information."

"Chittammai this, Chittammai that. The way you hung around her, like a toddler clinging around one's knees."

"Jealous, are you?" I tried to needle her.

"Not that you've done anything with all that material either."

"I will, I most certainly will, so help me god."

"I'll believe it when I see it." Chikkamma snorted, louder this time. Then she said with sudden passion, "It has to be written down, her story, my story, not to boost our vanity. Ah, what need of any name or fame do we have? But for the future, so young girls will know and remember the way things were. Do you think I haven't seen how older women are treated, yes, even by the likes of you. Yes, even here. Yes, even in those feminist gatherings and vigils you go to: I have seen them, the women of an earlier age ignored by the young women and patronized by your generation."

I gasped. Chikkamma had been around, unbeknownst to me. How could she know so much?

Then, as suddenly as she had appeared, Chikkamma decided to go for a nap. "If I am gone by the time you return from your shopping, just remember what I've told you. And note that I am watching."

"Please, Chikkamma, what's the hurry? I thought you'd stay with me a few days. Halfway around the world, and you still fly in and out the same way you used to forty years ago: I remember how you never stopped even for a cup of coffee, and how often you made Mother so exasperated trying to get you to stay for lunch or tiffin. In and out like lightning."

"So why should I change now, hnh?"

"So where are you going to be? With Aunt Meena, I suppose, your favourite always."

"Jealous, are you?" Chikkamma laughed her short delighted snorty laugh and went into the guest room, leaving me just a little breathless.

Four

Chikkamma set me back on the writing track all right. However, it was not about the maple leaf but about the Ashoka Chakra on the tricolour. I jotted down all kinds of anecdotes, and frequently tried to concentrate on Chikkamma's story. Chikkamma was here to stake her claim. Whoa, I thought, gratified at her trust in my writing skills. Her life was an enigma. Why did she do what she did? I should surely be able to understand this woman who was way ahead of her times. At a time when girls were married off at twelve, she had stayed unmarried till twenty five, had gone all the way to a Master's degree, and had become a principal of a girls' school. And then she had fallen in love with a married man. My imagination had to figure out how and why; and then she had done other things, even more incomprehensible. She continued to be as elusive as ever.

No, I couldn't even write notes on it to go back to when I have time. It had to be just right or it had better not be written at all. I had gone over her life many many times, totally captivated by her charisma that had hung over me all these years, even though she, like Professor and Chittammai, had intimidated me into awe during my growing years. What a colourful family I had had. Yes, I've got to write about them, had to. But the moment I came to that point of "had to," imagination and will power fled. January turned to February to March. One day, after one of the roadblocks to reach Chikkamma, I took a detour and decided I'd go on a shopping spree.

In the blinding sunshine refracting off white snow, I smiled to myself. Chikkamma, how real she seemed, sitting in that recliner, straight-backed as always, in her generic checkered sari. Her short snorty laugh. Were she alive, she'd be ninety years old. I wished I'd got to know her better. But when one is young, one doesn't see or hear, or rather one sees and hears things that are no big deal at all, like the faintly musty smell of Chittammai's clothes, as though they had not quite dried, and the raspy pitch of Chikkamma's voice and her dry sarcasm that seemed like whiplashes instead of being taken as mere acerbic humour. On the other hand, why should I think Chikkamma had not been real? There are more things on heaven and earth than your philosophy dreams of, Horatio. Maybe I had touched some magical key and opened worlds one does not normally see. Maybe Chikkamma was real and would stay with me.

And then I became a scientist's wife, a scientist's niece again. What would Professor say to my arguing with myself about my hallucinations? God, what a time to go mad, with Siv in his mid-fifties, no, I could not afford to see Chikkamma sitting in my living room, however wonderful it had been. But there was no harm seeing her as long as one knew it wasn't for real. Okay, that seemed a good compromise. Like Siv and his one hundred thousand Gayatris. He knew there was no magic but he would experiment anyway. Can one ever conduct a valid experiment if one goes in with an opinion already made?

Instead of stopping at the mall, I drove on towards Gatineau. I would take a look at the cottage, another of Siv's wildly extravagant deals, made after due thought so he said. But I knew better. He was fifty-four. Better a lemon of a cottage than a bosomy research assistant. However, it could be both: aye, there's the rub.

True, Siv had talked to me about the cottage on one of my first trips last fall, but he had a way of managing to do exactly what he wanted but making it appear like he had consulted me. Might be a nice place to come to when we retire, he said. Which gave me a jolt. For twenty-five years I had followed him Alcestis-like from Madras to Manipeg to Calgary to Ottawa assuming we'd go back to our Madras home once he retired. More recently, now that some of my friends were close to retirement age, they had said, Wake up and smell the coffee, Maru, you are never going back, not with all your children here and, in time, grandchildren. But I had my stock response: we had come away from our parents and we went back to visit them as often as our siblings who lived in India did, and my children would likewise come to visit me wherever we were. Huh, they said, have you considered the expense? It had nothing to do with expense. People always said that but I have kept tab of the ticket prices vis-à-vis the way we spent money here. It was twelve hundred dollars round trip in the Sixties, then it went down to four hundred and fifty dollars in the Seventies, and then up again to fifteen hundred now. Factor in the cost of the dollar then and now, and it is a lot more affordable than in the Sixties. Moreover, these same people will spend ten thousand dollars redoing their kitchen or living room without batting an eye, and spend three hundred dollars for the booze for their monthly parties, but going to India once in five years they think would be a drain on their finances.

We went to Madras more often than my brother-in-law who lived in Chandigarh, and his kids hardly knew my in-laws or spoke our language. But I didn't blame them, my brother-in- law and his wife, I mean. Maybe life is a lot more difficult in India. I say maybe because I don't want to be patronizing and assume it is, that's another attitude we expatriates fall into — being patronizing about folks back home. Bottom line is that some people visit their parents and some don't, and distance had nothing to do with it, nor money most times because it is a question of priorities — new carpets or a visit to one's parents.

We had a flat in Madras, once. When we wanted to sell it, the boys had made a to-do: keep it, they said, it would come in handy for them. I could see they were attached to it in an emotional way that had nothing to do with the realities of life. What would they know about everyday living in India, they who visited once in a while and were treated like VIPs by the family?

It wasn't for them I insisted we keep the flat, but for ourselves. After Siv retired, we'd go there, back to our roots, to Mylapore by the sea. But here was Siv buying a cottage near Meech Lake. For heavens' sake, why Meech, that godforsaken cesspool of our politicians' plots?

But I admit I was rather taken up with it when he drove me there. It was not on the beach, we are not beach kind of people, but a good mile or two inland, on a two acre plot. It was tucked away on top of a little hill. There was a rocky road meandering up to the one-room log cabin perched at the top, with the front door opening to the ground and the back door opening ten steps from the ground. It was a large room, a good thirty feet front to back, and though I am no architect, I could see it was an architect's dream putty: oh, the things one could do with that natural slope! But it had no water. And Siv had assigned me the job of finding water. We could pull in electricity from the country road farther up, where there was a motel open May to October, but getting a waterline was out of the question. Siv didn't think it was a problem. Don't lose sleep over it, he said, in this day and age, digging a bore well is easy.

So there we were, with a cottage in the middle of nowhere, with no water to be had for love or money, and a white elephant piece of real estate. The boys loved the idea: Giri said the area was bound to become a tourist paradise one day, and all we had to do was to wait till some developers came along and brought a waterline. But Siv wanted the cottage developed, now. He is one of those who worked to deadlines: if something was to be done by a certain date, he did it with time to spare. Not that I want to downgrade his talents, but it was mainly his obsession with deadlines that got things done: since he hand-picked clones, his students and assistants were also sticklers for deadlines. Now it was my job to find someone who could find water and drill a bore well. And someone else who would come up with floorplans that suited us. All before autumn. "The Yellow Pages," Siv said, as though they held all the secrets of the earth.

I almost lost my way. As I drove past one of the spots with a historical marker sign, I realized I'd forgotten the details, and I was upset by it. How could I forget the name of the family after whom that lake was named? How could I forget the interesting story about some algae that grew there that either killed everything or supported life in a miraculous way? God, what was the story? I was surely lost. I had shown that lake to so many of Siv's foreign visitors, and added my story of our trip to Jamaica, one of my favourites.

I had gone with Siv to a conference in Jamaica, and as with conferences everywhere, they had arranged a sightseeing trip. As the bus rounded a bend up a hill, everyone in the bus gasped, for there below us was a lake with resplendent colours, purple and turquoise and pink, the waves shimmering in the sun. And then came the tour guide's measured voice: the colours were due to the waste from the bauxite refinery half a mile up. A quiver of guilt passed through the bus, for of course as with every conference in any of these exotic places, half the delegates were from Canada, and we all knew the stake Canada had in the Caribbean bauxite industry.

As I turned round a bend, I saw the lookout: I was not lost. Soon I came to Meech Lake. At the familiar sight, the details came back. The small lake back there was green because of the natural algae around, the septic tanks from real estate developments had polluted the water but there were two levels of water, which did not mix — the merimictetic phenomenon. And the green lake was called Pink Lake because the area was owned by the Pink family.

Third turn to the left, up the dirt road for a mile and a half and there it was, at an elevation. Our cottage. To remodel this place would cost a fortune, because, of course, one had to keep the old ambience.

Whether we remodelled or not, we needed to get a water supply. A cabin without running water was unheard of in this day in this place. No wonder it had been on the market forever until a sucker like Siv came along.

I said as much to our neighbour, who walked to where I was. He was a young man, and I had to look at him twice before I figured out what was odd about him — he had wide-legged pants of some silky material, a kind of gaberdine that was in vogue in the Fifties. As was the cut of the trousers. Yes, trousers, very British. We greeted each other, and because I was thirsty by now, I was glad to see him. I usually take a bottle of Evian when I go anywhere other than the mall, but since the mall was all I had meant to go to today, I didn't have any. I told him what I thought of a lot without water and how thirsty I was. He nodded. He thumbed towards a rainbarrel behind him. He helped take the lid off and I cupped some water into my mouth. "Thank you," I said.

"Welcome," he said, and took out a pipe. Again, I could not but notice there was something arcane about a young man in baggy trousers smoking a pipe. He seemed so British.

"Have you been to India?" I asked him, and then bit my tongue. What a stupid thing to say. Now, if he were older, it might have made sense. The number of older men who said they'd been in India during the war never ceased to amaze me. "Chai lao," they'd say, or "Boy, chhota peg lao," and I would laugh politely.

"Yes," he said. He tapped the pipe and took out a thingummy to clean it; then he took out a pouch and set about filling tobacco in the pipe; after which he put it between his lip, without lighting it, and said, "I died there."

"Of the heat, eh?" I said, "what places did you visit?"

"Just Lucknow, we were garrisoned in Lucknow."

That threw me for a loop.

"Did you enjoy yourself?"

"She was a little thing, just fourteen probably, Amina was her name, and she insulted the captain by slapping him instead of giving in, and so we were ordered to rape her. Lots were drawn for the sequence, and we went in one by one into the tent, while others gawped from peepholes. I was the last. I held her in my arms but the captain barked that orders are orders. She died in my arms. If you can call that enjoying."

I looked away. Why was he saying this? I shivered. Was he a psychopath? It started to snow. "I'd better get back before it starts blowing," I said, making my escape.

I told Siv about this weird experience. He looked at me from above his reading glasses, and said, "That's odd. I've met him a couple of times — no pipe, no baggy trousers — his name is Roger something, Roger Janzen, I think, fortyish, I would say. And he has no water either. And DON'T go to these places except during midday, simple rule ..." he stopped. He was about to say rule of thumb, an old habit, but I had educated him on how the phrase originally pertained to the law that men could whip their wives as long as the switch was no thicker than their thumb.

Next day, when I was dusting my tall bronzes of Siva and Parvati that we had mounted in the wall cabinet in the living room, I noticed something. The lithograph of "The Last Supper," that we had mounted to hide the patch where the owners had removed one of their paintings, had slipped to the floor, not broken, thank god, but it was sitting on the floor. The cleaning woman came only every other week, which is why I was dusting, and Siv said of course not, he never touched anything. Which I knew anyway, from the dust that collected in our suite of rooms, where the cleaning woman never went. Siv did not like strange people in his living area.

I wanted a rational explanation. Siv said he would look into anchoring the lithograph more securely that weekend, and that we should be glad nothing had broken. Then, seeing I was not satisfied, he said with a twinkle in his eye that maybe it was a simple message from the bronzes that were saying, I am the Lord thy God and thou shalt not have any other gods before me.

You are not serious, I looked at him accusingly. He said he didn't know whether he was serious, but knew he was not facetious. He said he had completed forty thousand Gayatris as of yesterday.

I felt queasy. "I don't like it," I said, "first Chikkamma, then that British soldier from the World War, and now this."

"So far, all can be rationally explained," he said. "Our neighbour was just trying to spook you; the nail just happened to come loose; and Chikkamma? You've long been obsessed with your two great aunts. Which reminds me, Ukkal is back in town. Do you think we should invite him to our party that is coming up?"

Seeing my blank look, he explained, "The biographer guy you realized too late you did not like."

"You didn't either, so why bother?" I said.

"True, but he has invited himself already," he said, "and will keep pushing for a formal invitation till he gets it. Just be more careful, this time. Biographers nowadays have no compunction whatsoever."

That first evening of my return, we had spent two hours with Ukkal and that was two hours too many. In my usual light-hearted way, while waiting for the entrée, which was taking forever, I had told him a few anecdotes about Professor. Off the record, I said. I wanted him to know something of the human side of this great man who was either over-venerated or over-slandered in most of the stories that appeared in the media at his death. This urge to get it right, to get into the shoes and soul of our subjects, to get the essence, Siv and I had talked about it often enough. Siv wasn't into reading fiction and poetry but he certainly was into biography; he even puts himself on the waiting list in the public library to get a hold of new biographies. "All lives are interesting," he's said, "as long as the subject is dead." Now, with this man who claimed he had family letters and the family's blessing on his project, we wanted him to get the essence of his subject. Yes, the mad genius hated politicians and refused to let the Prime Minister visit his lab.Yes, he had turned away all women from being his students when he was director of the Science Institute. Yes, he had busts and photographs of himself all over the campus. But what was his reason, motivation, goals? More important, what was he holistically, as a whole human being? Once one got the essence of the man, one could not go wrong, Siv maintained. Just by being with us, talking to us, maybe this Ukkal could get a feel for his subject that mere written records could not.

I did not relate the story of the Nobel Laureate's midnight yells, but I did say how he phoned home one afternoon for a pillow to be sent pronto, no, make it two. Chittammai tore two pillows off the bed and we rushed posthaste in the old Studebaker to the lab because once in a while Professor got an ache in the small of his back — another of the things that made him yell like he was being murdered — his treatment was to stack a couple of soft pillows against the back of his chair, then keep working. When we got there, he was perfectly all right. He grabbed the pillows, pressed them over the telephone, and then stalked off back to his experiment without saying another word. Another time, and this was one of our family favourites, a British scientist, a titled one at that, was visiting the lab. Professor, as usual, had left for the lab at eight o'clock; Chittammai, as usual, had patiently waited for the guest to wake up; had overseen that the servant boy had taken him morning tea and hot water for his bath etc.; had sat with him at the breakfast table; and had brought him to the lab at ten o'clock as scheduled. But Professor was nowhere to be found. Nor were any of his research assistants — of whom he had five at the time — anywhere to be found. So Chittammai played host and took him around the various labs. Over the years, she had become an expert tourguide, and a more diplomatic one than Professor, who tended to air his opinions of politicians more bluntly than was politic. Having come to the end of her innovativeness at keeping up small talk with this very pompous earl, she figured she would take him to the gem-collection room. Since Professor's major research was in light refraction and diffusion, he had an awesome collection of gems, especially diamonds.

She opened the door to the room, and the earl held it open for her, ladies first. Which was just as well. She took one look, said in Tamil, "Uh, oh, what is this clownery?" and then stepped back, closing the door, "They are not here either, let us try the Boardroom. I seem to remember they had an early morning meeting there," and she led him away.

They had been in the gem room, as a matter of fact, a room that was usually kept dark so the gems would glow. They were all there, five research assistants, two lab technicians, and Professor, all stripped to their briefs: three were on their knees running their hands over the floor; two were emptying all the pockets of all the clothes thrown on the table; and two in the act of pulling down their trousers; while Professor stood like an African king amidst them, flashlight in hand. They had been working with the stones and, when they set about adjourning in order to meet the visitor, the count did not tally — one of the bigger diamonds was missing, hence the stripping.

Ukkal had listened to the stories, nodding sagely from time to time. He did not laugh. At that point, we should have known he was trouble.

Sure enough, two days later the story came back to us from another source with some garbled commentary that Ukkal had added, making Professor more a clown than the eccentric genius he was. Perhaps I was responsible. It was the first time I had narrated the story in any language but the original Tamil, and though I enjoyed my own narration, clearly something had been missed. The story was really more about Chittammai, and I should have told him that. How could one translate Chittammai's "Uh, oh" and communicate her masterful presence of mind in a new language to someone who had never met her or Professor? Maybe that is why none of his students ever wrote about him, and maybe that is why there was so much misreading of his words and actions. Maybe that too was the reason the coterie of his students and assistants seemed so hermeneutical to outsiders, such a closed group. When I said all this to Siv one evening, he looked at me over his reading glasses and said, "Now you know why the Gayatri is whispered by the mentor into the disciple's ear and the initiated student has to swear on all things most sacred to him that he would not pass it on to the uninitiated. The truth in untrained hands becomes untruth."

Chikkamma. I wished she would come back. But now, more than ever, I felt I could not, even should not, put anything on paper.

"So," Siv said, in bed that night, "do you think some of the Gayatri power has rubbed off on me, some tejas you could feel shooting from me to you?" "Okay, okay," I said, "all those moans and ahs were just to make you feel good."

Yes, it was good. Maybe there was something to this Gayatri power thing. Better this obsession with the Gayatri than with some shapely brunette. Unless, of course, it was both.

Five

When I heard that Ukkal had invited himself, I stopped thinking of our party as a fun thing. It became a chore that had to be completed. So I rashly invited a few others as well, thinking, I might as well clean my slate of all social responsibilities for a while once this was over. The guest list was a jumble of disparate people, and growing by the day.

Meanwhile, I went every day with a different contractor to check out possibilities for the cottage. I never saw the young man again, nor the other that Siv had met. Near the back entrance is a smooth rock just the right height for a seat. I sat on it while the estimator walked around with his writing pad and measuring tape, taking notes. It is remarkable how similar these contractors are in their work habits. I suppose they go through some course same as secretaries have their training schools.

Lakes at every bend in the road but nary a vein of water anywhere on our two acres. Three diviners had come and gone, and one professional company that cost as much for their professional expertise as I thought a bore well would have cost. They gave their verdict, however, in no uncertain terms. There was no water on our land. However, they could draw a line from another place, just a mile down the road, where their affiliated building contractors were putting up a cabin. They would do all the paperwork necessary with the city, with the owners of another plot through which the pipe would have to run, with anything else necessary. Go for it, Siv told me, though I cringed at the figure on their estimate sheet.

Water, no wonder most wars in the desert were over watering holes: oases; little lakes that were dry six months of the year. Hunger one could cope with but not with thirst. There is a story of a Moghul emperor, before he became emperor, walking through the desert with his pregnant wife, who is said to have slashed his horse to death and fed her the blood, any liquid for their parched throats. There is a story in Hindu lore about God teaching a proud Brahmin how to get out of the stranglehold of caste — God trapped the man in a waterless desert and then sent a tanner, the lowest of the low, with a leather flask slung around his neck along with a dead animal he had killed, and the Brahmin gratefully held the tanner's hand and drank from the leather flask swinging against the dead animal. Water. Where were we to get water?

I walked down a rock path away from both cottages. Through a clearing I saw the next hillock. On it was a temple, a Hanuman temple, the red triangular flag waving in the early spring breeze. There were Hanuman monkeys in the tall trees, their bodies covered with brilliant grey fur, their long tails swinging proudly, their sharp beady eyes shining from their little black faces. I remembered them in Chittammai's garden, plucking green mangoes and dropping them near the watchman who already had a tough time chasing little urchins off the jackfruit and mango trees. Once, when a baby monkey died, the whole congregation of them had sat silently on the branches, even their tails hanging motionlessly, while the mother held the little one and whimpered quietly.

The estimator gave me his papers, and we went our different ways. As I drove back, I wondered desperately what all these people were trying to tell me. The monkey remembrance had an immediate effect. I went into a tizzy of worry over my children: were they happy? were they in good health? what did the future hold for them? That evening, I phoned each of them and talked all evening. Kathy was doing well. Arvind was trying to submit his thesis before the baby came. Giri and Nari were impatient with my mother hen clucking.

A few days later, I was at the spice store on Bank Street when I had one of those happenstance meetings that open doors. There was a grey-haired man with a mahogany walking stick, which rightaway placed him as a visitor from the subcontinent. He was with a young woman, a white woman, who was earnestly talking to Raj Shah, the store owner, on how best to use the package of sambar powder she had in her hand. On seeing me, Raj told her I would be the best person to advise her, and introduced me. Hearing my obviously Tamil name, the old man perked up rightaway. "Namaskaram, amma," he said greeting me, and continued in Tamil, "How are you? It is so wonderful to be able to talk in Tamil to someone." We chatted: he was visiting his son; it was his first visit; he had worked as a clerk in the Postal Services and had just retired. His son had been calling him for so long and now that he had all the time in the world, he had come. This was a beautiful place: no wonder his son had not returned to India; who would, after a taste of this affluent society? But the taste of the foods, ah that was another matter. All so bland, poor child, she tries hard, she is a sweet child but how can she know anything about sambar and rasam? His voice trailed: I could see his tongue was remembering the feel of tamarind and ground coriander.

Rightaway I invited him home. I had made idlis for breakfast, and yes, he must come with me. I spoke to his daughter-in-law, and she was hesitant. But I insisted. “Come along,” I said, “It won’t take long.” She asked me if I lived nearby. No place is too far, I said, you know Rockcliffe, don’t you?

“Thank you so much,” she said, “but some other time, maybe?” There was something in her tone that made me wonder if I had said Rockcliffe the way people who live there often do, with that certain inflection. I hastened to be even more cordial. “Please, please do come.” She said she had to be home for the children’s lunch break. But that was a whole two hours away. We dithered back and forth and at last she agreed that I could take her father-in-law home and drop him back.

In the car, as I was backing out of the lot, he said, “She was a great cook,” and I realized he was remembering his wife and that she was dead, and I was even gladder I had met him. “She never let me cook at home,” he said, “Did you ever think of how all the festivities-cooks are always men? I have cooking in my blood, you know, but I went in for the security of a government job.” As he spoke on, I discovered he was the son of Sripati Iyer, our family’s master cook, who had been in charge of every wedding lunch and dinner for years. That made my day. What a small world. And when I switched on the cassette, which had Lalgudi Jayaraman’s violin, his day was made. He sat back, closed his eyes, his fingers kept beat on his thigh, and there were the “ha, ahh,” and shaking of head of a true *rasika.*

We made other family connections over idlis and coffee. Given such a gourmet guest, I exerted myself and made good Madras coffee, bringing milk to the boil and giving an expresso whisk at the end so the top frothed over. It was a treat for him, I could see.

As we chatted, I poured out some of my problems, and when I came to our waterless cottage, he jumped up. “I knew the moment I saw you that I would come alive,” he said, “God’s ways are known only to him, praise be. He has given me a purpose.”

Turned out he was a water diviner! He wanted to set out that minute. “Wednesday is an auspicious day,” he said, “Let’s go. We must be there by noon." I told him that was not possible, it was an hour's drive. "Well, let us leave at one-thirty," he said, settling back to his third cup of coffee, "after Rahu passes."

I made the necessary phone calls — to his daughter-in-law saying that I would drive him home after five, and to Siv that I may not be in till six from the cottage. Siv wasn't there and I knew better than to tell him, or his secretary who took most messages, that I had someone who claimed to be a water diviner and that we could not leave before one-thirty because on Wednesdays Rahu, the obstacle guy in the sky, ruled from noon to one-thirty.

Mr. Chinnadurai Iyer, that is his name, asked if there were trees where we were going, and I said, "Yes, there were many." Next, he wanted to know if there would be a handsaw where we were going. He needed it to cut a divining rod. I went to the worktable in the basement and brought one upstairs. At one-forty-five (it is always better to give Rahu a wide berth), we set off.

Once there, the affable old man got transformed. He took the handsaw, tested it with his finger, honed it on my rock-seat, and smiled. It was a weird smile, a "Ah, ha, I've got you now" smile, and I shivered with some trepidation. Anything could happen, I thought. If something untoward happened: if that young man in the Fifties trousers turned up; or Chikkamma; or the monkeys. I was going batty. I'd know it but there was nothing I could do about it. Maybe this man was also like them, not real. But they were, and so was he, whether of flesh and not, who cared? To get water for the cottage, one had to accept gifts from wherever they came.

"It is better if you stay in the house, lady," he said, "You know what our rules say. Ladies had best stay in."

The feminist in me flared up. But since he still had the handsaw, I put on the naive student act, "Oh, because we are weak, unclean vessels?"

He looked surprised. "Ammamma, all our rules are directed at men, so the weak ones can concentrate on their work and not walk the stars. Don't you know how even the perfume from a woman's dress can distract a man to madness? Also, when the spirit rises, we are not a pleasant sight."

I must admit that though I was pleased with what he said, I was glad I did not have to be with him. He walked towards the trees, and I saw him testing branches, lopping off a few, discarding them, going farther, away from my view. I waited, hoping someone would appear, Chikkamma, maybe Chittammai this time, the monkeys, the soldier.

But the house was within the protected circle, I guess, and no one came.

It was almost an hour before Mr. Iyer returned. He clapped for me from way off, and waited till I joined him. He then took me to the spot he had marked and said, "Dig here, at fifty feet you will come to dirty water; go deeper, another twenty, thirty feet, and you will get water sweeter than any you can get from any tap or well anywhere in the city." With stones and twigs and leaves, he marked out the area, sticking a twig where the X would be.

"Don't take too long," he said, "the wind could be strong up here."

That evening, I told Siv all about my day's adventures. "Go for it," he said. "We could go first thing in the morning, if you wish to mark it in a more secure way."

"You mean you'd take his word and get the rig out there? They charge by the centimetre at that depth, you know."

"Look how much you've saved by paying him with a plate of idlis," he said.

We went back next day and planted markers. I phoned Iyer several times, just to make sure he would still be around and willing when the digging rig people were ready to come out.

We went back two Saturdays later. At forty-eight feet, Chuck, the bore-well man, jumped back, "I'll be darned, all that trouble and look what we get."

I looked at Iyer. Iyer looked at Siv and nodded. Siv looked at Chuck and nodded, keep going.

At fifty-five feet, Chuck said, It is solid rock, wanna keep going?

I could see the digits being added to the invoice, but Siv kept nodding, keep going. They had to add a special augur to dig through rock. At seventy-nine feet, huzza, more miraculous than Old Faithful, we had our water, clear and sweet as from Athabasca.

When we took Iyer back to our house for lunch, he followed me to the kitchen, as I was putting things away. "How long have you been here?" he asked. I told him. He sniffed around the kitchen; he circled the living room, standing a long while in front of "The Last Supper" which I had remounted in its old place.

"What is above this?" he asked.

"One of the closets?" I hazarded a guess.

"Something bad is here," he said, "you must find out what it is and remove it." Again he had that scary, glazed look.

Sivaram, having finished his coffee, prepared to leave for his lab.

Saturday was the day he worked longest, since it was the most peaceful day, without telephones and meetings and people.

"Oh, my husband has to leave," I said, "Maybe he could drop you off on his way."

But Siv, so like him not to take a hint, cordially shouted, "Take your time, Mr. Iyer. Have another cup of Maru's excellent coffee. She can drop you any time you want. " And away he went.

Iyer did have another cup of coffee, and was again his affable self. He looked wistfully at the kitchen and said he wished he could make some sense of all the gadgets, and maybe then he could start cooking, maybe for a restaurant. Were there any idli-dosa restaurants in the city? I was at ease by now, and we chatted about Indian restaurants and the lack of South Indian cuisine. He interrupted me mid-sentence and asked, "Where is your *pooja* room? Sometimes, people have the worst possible things in the *pooja* room, thinking it is doing them good."

I couldn't tell him I didn't have a prayer room any more than I could admit to anyone else that I did not have a microwave. Lamely I said, "As I said, I've been here only a little while and I haven't quite set things up the way they should be."

"Something is bad here," he said, got up and again started sniffing walls and doors. Again he stood in front of "The Last Supper." "What is under this?" he said.

"Just the basement ceiling, I guess," I said, "maybe you'd like to check it out " I showed him the staircase. I didn't like the look in his eyes.

He came up in a few minutes. "No, nothing there, must be upstairs." He started walking towards the stairs. "Yes," he shouted as he neared the top, "Yes, I can feel it, yes." He disappeared into the study. I raced up: Siv hated strangers coming upstairs.

Iyer stood in front of the hologram. "Good," he said, approvingly, "Good, your husband is a good man. Does his Gayatri Japam regularly."

How did he know that? I was positive that the hologram was not any standard symbol or sign because Siv had said it was his own interpretation of the piece that the sidewalk artist had painted right in front of his eyes, and yet Iyer seemed to recognize it.

Iyer went on to the next room, my room, which had not only my papers and books but a whole lot of junk that I threw in from time to time, every time I had to clean the living room in a hurry, usually when Siv phoned to say he was bringing guests home for tea. Old magazines and newspapers, mainly, but also many unpacked boxes of my books and notebooks that I had collected for my magnum opus.

Iyer was in a frenzy now. His arms were stretched in a curve in front of him, and he was grunting and muttering, It is here, whatever it is is right here somewhere. His eyes rolled and turned red I swear. He was walking like a chimpanzee, knees and elbows bent, bow-legged, his snout thrust out. "Open this," he ordered me, tapping one of the cartons with a ruler he had picked up from the table, as though he didn't want to touch any infernal thing. I opened it. He poked the ruler around, and said, "No, open the next." That didn't turn up anything either. "Next." I had to pull the carton off the wall in order to pry it open. Yes, yes, yes, he shouted, bobbing up and down like a monkey, "Yes, yes." He made me take every single thing out, including much to my embarrassment a bra that had somehow got stuck between two envelopes in which I had stashed old cheques. There was a large brown envelope at the bottom: "Yes, yes, yes."

In it was a painting given to me by one of Chittammai's leeches, as we called the young foreigners who somehow turned up at her door, claiming some connection to someone who had stayed with her at some other time. The hippies of the Sixties had likely set up a network of how to feed off whom. Chittammai always welcomed them, and let them stay in the two-room cottage at the end of the eastern wall of her house. This painting had been done by a young man with a long name he had adopted — Siddhavilasacharya. I was there, with another cousin that Chittammai had borrowed for the summer, when these two stayed at the cottage — a lean young man and his leaner wife, all skin and bones, but with lustrous eyes that bowled us away. They wore the saffron robes of mendicants and we — teenagers at the time, whispered to each other, "Do they? Don't they?" And answered ourselves, "Some real sparks must be flying when they do." They had that aura about them. In hindsight, it probably came from their jaundiced paleness, for jaundice was an illness that nomadic foreigners often picked up, but at the time we thought they had some spiritual aura, so intensely sincere were they in everything they did. Every evening, they chanted some monotonous lines, and by the time they were through, our ears buzzed with a tune that followed us into bed.

He had given to me, as gift, one of his paintings. It was a Sri Chakra, beautifully symmetrical, all hand drawn with coloured pens, every line, every arc in proportion. He truly did have artistic skills. I had put it away, meaning to frame it but never had. When researching for one of my television shows, I had read up a lot about the Sri Chakra — how the geometrical design was the first step in any architectural structure, how the stone etched with it was placed on the ground with prayers that it hold up the whole edifice, how the main pillar, the sacred *sthamba* of a temple, rose directly on it etc. etc. I had read too that the Sri Chakra was too powerful to be in homes, that if anyone did have it at home, they should follow a very rigidly prescribed code of rites associated with it.

"Who gave it to you?" he asked.

"Some old friend, long ago. He and his wife were very nice people."

"Couldn't have been," he said, "Not properly trained. The kind who can turn truths to lies, good to evil, without meaning to, I grant, but they are not good. Get rid of it. Don't tear it up because that would disperse it as the wind disperses pollen. Don't burn it, for the wind might carry the ashes. Don't even throw it in a well because it would pollute the water for a thousand years. And don't keep it at home."

"But we've had it all these years," I remonstrated.

"There is a germinating period for evil as for good: nothing springs full blown into the world. It has perhaps only recently come into its time. It is not too late. Throw it into running water far from everywhere, or bury it deep, deep in the earth."

He seemed totally worn out. He went down the steps, stretched himself right there in the hallway and closed his eyes. I tiptoed to the living room, sat on the recliner, and waited.

He woke up in half an hour. "It's been a long day, amma," he said, "If you don't mind, I would like to go home now." He said it in a meek voice, like a child who was apologizing for a tantrum. I packed up some idlis and sambar for him, and dropped him back. In the car, I put on a Balamurali tape. His fingers kept beat for the first minute and then he must have fallen asleep. Sara, his daughter-in-law, whom he called Sarada, was on the porch. "We went to the Gatineau," I said, "I'm afraid it's been a long day for him." She nodded. I gave her the brown bag, "Something he liked," I said apologetically, "Maybe your husband might like it too, and you."

"Thank you," she said, "You are very kind. He looks forward to your phone calls."

How much do they know, I thought as I went back to the car, of this man's preternatural skills?

I would have told Siv all about these strange happenings, but when I returned there was a message on the phone. Siv was bringing home some German scientists.

By the time we went to bed that night, I figured I would just quietly get rid of the painting, drop it in Pink Lake along with the toxins that had already polluted it? I came from a family of scientists, was wife and mother of scientists: no, this Sri Chakra thing was just a bit too much. I had had it for years, and nothing had happened. Now it had the power to knock "The Last Supper" off the wall below it? — yes, the box had been precisely directly above the picture frame — it was too much. I wouldn't bother about it. Besides, Siv seemed worried about some high-level negotiation that was going on about some international partnership in a wind-tunnel project that no one was supposed to talk about and that had to be signed by the end of the week. Sri Chakra, bah.

But I could not forget how like a monkey Mr. Iyer looked as he jumped up and down, ruler in hand. Maybe he had met up with my monkeys up at the cottage. Maybe that is why he didn't want me following him. Maybe he was a monkey. Or, oh my goodness, maybe the monkeys had abducted him and come in his shape and poor Iyer was still up in the Gatineau. I argued myself into a ludicrous corner.

The following week, I told Siv about the Sri Chakra episode. "You've had it for years," he said, "one of those things you've been toting around from before we were married."

"I could say the same of your hologram," I said.

"Peace," he said, "to each their own."

"So what should I do with it?" I asked.

"Do what he told you to do," he said. "It will please him and we do owe him big time."

"But it can't be torn, burnt, thrown in standing water, so where do I get rid of it?"

"Bury it like he said, our yard is big enough."

"That is too close, what if the curse comes in through the patio doors?"

"Don't laugh at things you don't know anything about."

"You don't believe in all this, please tell me you don't."

"No, of course I don't, but you know you are no good at lying, and Iyer is going to be after you asking just what you did with it. So you might as well bury it the way he said."

I fully meant to get rid of the Sri Chakra, but got caught up in the daily routine.

Routine. How annoying that can be at times, and at other times how reassuring. The m.m. syndrome had receded to the background. I didn't want to say it had gone away, for one always had to be alert for signs, but it didn't seem to be there.

Six

"Wednesday already. It is really time to start working on my party," I told Siv next day at breakfast. "Do you think I can get it all ready in two days?" I was worried. "Oh, you will, you are a pro at all this," Siv said. I went over the guest list as he sat at his morning crossword. "Isn't this rather more than we usually have?" Siv asked.

"About twice as many," I said.

"Don't overwork yourself, Maroo my Maroo," he said, "just get it catered."

"No way," I said, "All the appetizers and desserts are coming from Haveli's and I'll whip up my usual pilaf and chickpea curry and a couple of dry veggies. You'll take care of the drinks, as usual."

"Done it already. You have twenty more on the guest list than I bought for last week, but I have a lot of wine left over from Christmas. Parties are for intellectual exchange and/or fun and laughter, not for guzzling beer and wolfing down food. I wish you women wouldn't kill yourselves cooking."

Siv said it every time we planned or went to a party, but he was a wolfer, whether he had ever thought about it or not. "Don't worry," I said, "it is just the mother hen syndrome in us, we like to see people enjoy the food we cook. My job is no problem: yours is, making sure that they don't go tipsy on us."

That afternoon, he called just as I'd sat down to draw up a list of all the details that had to be seen to for Friday's party.

"Maroo my Maroo, what would I do without you?" I knew he had something big he was forcing on me. "Let me guess," I said, "the Liechtenstein delegation wants us to go to the moon this evening."

"Close enough" he said, "we might get overnight guests." I knew his "might" was only for form, that he had already invited whoever it was.

"You'll like him," he said. "His name is Sam White and he is a music historian. Nirmala e-mailed me from Delhi —Nirmala is one of Professor's last students." That said it all. Siv had not met this woman, Nirmala, but it was a fraternity thing. One could not refuse a favour asked by a fellow student of Professor's.

"Sure," I said. "No problem. Music historian, eh?"

"Yes, Carnatic music, from what I understand. Should be interesting. And, oh, by the way, he has a kid with him, some Malayali boy he's adopted, who takes care of him. Nirmala said Sam needs help at night."

"Is he terminally ill or something? Please, no."

"No, no, I had lunch with him. Is healthy as a horse."

I set about getting the guest room ready. We have two guest rooms upstairs, separated by a good-sized bathroom which opens into both rooms and the hall. If it was an attendant who needed to be within hearing distance, I had best pull the camp cot into a guest room, good enough for a little Malayali boy, surely. I got sheets and towels: the public part of the house was clean enough because the cleaning woman comes alternate Tuesdays, and had come this week. My study was a mess, as usual, all the emptied cartons of the Sri Chakra episode still to be refilled. I quickly stuffed as much back into each carton as it would easily hold but that left a whole pile that would have gone in only if I had packed the cartons properly. I brought another carton from the basement and threw the remaining junk into it. The Sri Chakra envelope I placed at the very top of one of the packed cartons already in a corner so it wouldn't get creased, and stacked two of the cartons over it. Yes, it had to be gotten rid of but it was so pretty I didn't have the heart to crumple it. I placed the other cartons on the floor alongside those already against the wall and covered the row of cartons neatly with a pretty printed coverlet I'd bought in Jaipur on my last visit to India. Done. One of these days, very soon, I must get rid of the Sri Chakra. Just get the party over first. What insanity had made me invite fifty people? Saris and shirts had piled up in our bedroom, but that was okay. Private No Thoroughfare.

When I was eight, nine maybe, we went to Mysore and toured the Maharaja's palace. The government had long pensioned off all Maharajahs, but the opulence was still very much there. There were cars, maybe fifty of them, Rolls-Royces, big-backed Chevrolets and Fords, little sports cars, all with a lot of gold splashed across them, and the royal crest planted on the hood. And there were horses: having only seen the nags that pull the one-horse buggies on city streets, these horses that towered over us awed me. And then neverending halls with crystal chandeliers and larger-than-life paintings of royalty. At the end of one of the hallways was a large sign, "Private No Thoroughfare." The guide told us that the royal family lived on the other side of the door. The Royal Family. Wow. Later, when I read books by P.G. Wodehouse with earls taking two shilling six from visitors to their castle, the whole royal experience was brought to a place lower on the ladder. But the fact that someone could put up a sign "Private No Thoroughfare" and really ban anyone from entering, continued to be the ultimate rung of individualism. And Siv was born an individualist. One of the first things he had done after moving in was to put locks on all doors upstairs, all of which would have to be changed over again when our lease ended. I never locked my den, nor had any of our guests at any time as far as I knew. Siv's habit of locking up his study and our bedroom on party days was a nuisance, but I could go along with it. It said something, and I liked what it said, though some thought it was a show of distrust.

Siv brought the guests home. I greeted them and after small talk, went to the kitchen to get the coffee and snacks. The boy followed me.

"Is it all right to come in?" he said, and I said, "Of course."

"I'll make the coffee for Sami," he said in Tamil. "He wanted me to call him Sam, but how can I do that, no?" he said, smiling. "So I call him Swami/Sami." He had a lovely face.

"Have you been with him long?"

"About two years, now," he said. "Long enough to know my way around these kitchens. I'll take care of breakfast, too, please. Just tell me what I shouldn't do. Like if you don't like the smell of scrambled eggs in the kitchen, I could make boiled eggs. Same with onions or garlic, just tell me. And I could make breakfast for you too, amma sweet amma."

His name was Kitu, and Sam called him Kutty, little one. He was adorable-looking. Long silken lashes over soft almond-shaped eyes, his skin a smooth chocolate brown, beautiful sparkling teeth with just a hint of overlapping in the front two teeth, and a little bow-shaped mouth. He had wavy black hair. He should have been a girl, I thought to myself, so much beauty wasted on a boy.

But it wasn't really, as I found out next morning when I went into their room, thinking I would put in extra towels while they were at breakfast. His bed hadn't been slept in. So that was the help Sam needed.

Kitu, true to his word, had made breakfast, a delectable one of omelettes spiced with green chilies and onions, and skillet-toasted brown bread. Sam left with Siv, and Kitu hung about me, waiting to help. I took out fresh beans, and carrots. I might as well as get them chopped/peeled and bagged to save time tomorrow. We worked at the kitchen table, Kitu happily chatting about all the places he'd seen in the last two years. I must admit I felt a little queasy: he was a child and surely this was child exploitation. Just how old was he?

I asked him if he liked his work. "It is hardly work," he said, smiling. "Sam seems very fond of you," I said. "Oh yes," he said fervently, "Oh yes, he loves me so much. Look what he gave me last Friday in Toronto!" He ran upstairs and brought a Mondetta T-shirt and an Angora sweater. The Angora was a gift from when they were in Chicago two weeks ago. "I do like new clothes," he said happily.

I asked him where he grew up. He told me he was born in Guruvayur — that is where he met Sam. Sam was making a video of the temple procession. Of all the boys who crowded to get foreigners' attention, he had been the lucky one. Sam employed him to carry his equipment around, and the rest is history.

"Didn't his parents feel sad he was going away so far?" His answer was simple. His sister was only fifteen when she got married and she had to go away to Delhi.

"But that is still within the country," I said.

He said he had been on his own since he was twelve, away from his family though he had another one.

I said, "New York is so far away."

"The train from Delhi to Madras takes thirty-six hours but the plane from New York takes only sixteen," he said.

"You mean you've been back since then?"

"Oh yes. We go back every winter. Sami says he's never missed the music festival in twelve years. Last year we stayed two months, right up to the Tyagaraja Festival at Tiruvaiyaru."

"You are lucky," I said.

"Oh yes," he said, joining his palms in thanks to God, "oh yes, I am so lucky. Sami is so kind, and so gentle, always so gentle."

He said it with so much love, so much gratitude, I wanted to give him a hug.

He wanted to know the menu and when I told him, he seemed disappointed. He wanted to cook up a storm: "Why not *aviyal*? Let us make *aviyal*. In this country we can get fresh vegetables of every kind right through the year, isn't that wonderful? We'll put six different vegetables and grind fresh coconut and make an *aviyal*. Please, amma sweet amma?" He liked repeating the endearment he had coined for me.

"Okay, you can make it for the Saturday lunch. Let's go to the vegetable market now, shall we?"

He was utterly delighted at the fresh fruit and vegetable stalls at the market.

He picked up far more kinds of vegetables than we had use for, every kind of gourd he could see. "I don't have a fridge big enough for all this," I remonstrated, but he didn't think we'd need a fridge. "Everything will be cooked, eaten and digested tomorrow," he said, picking up three coconuts.

"Day after tomorrow," I said, "Saturday lunch, okay?"

"Can we make a fruit salad for tonight?" he pleaded. He was so sweet, one couldn't deny him anything. Fact was, all that I could see was a lovely girl, the one I never had.

"Okay, pick up whatever fruits you want."

"Amma, sweet amma, you just sit back all of today. I'll do it all."

As I drove to my next stop, the Indian spice store, I thought of Mr. Iyer. Maybe with Kitu around, he could learn to cook in a Canadian kitchen. I called him up from the store, because he lived in that area. I heard him speaking to Sara. He was so sorry, but he couldn't come today; he could come tomorrow, he was free all day tomorrow for sure. "No thanks," I said. "During the weekend, maybe," I said, "but not tomorrow." I could feel his disappointment even over the wires.

As I drove back, I thought of how I could maybe help Iyer start his restaurant. Haveli's had delicious masala dosai at their Sunday brunches, but competition was always good, kept one on one's toes. I would have to rethink that, I told myself, back to my m.m. syndrome. If one had to be on one's toes all the time, it affected one's creativity; one needed a certain stability if one had to be creative. I found myself repeating Siv's argument for tenure for university professors at a heated discussion at a recent party. Brian thought the whole tenure system should be abolished: mandatory retirement at sixty-five should be imposed, and all the old fogies who were sitting on their butts and collecting their hundred thou. a year should be sent packing. Siv's argument had seemed so level-headed and convincing at the time, but now I thought, so why didn't people apply the same precept to marriages? No unfaithfulness, no divorce, no m.m. problems. I could have actually worked on my "Maru and the Maple Leaf" in Manipeg, instead of worrying about m.m. and moving here.

My mind went back to Manipeg, to Alf A and Brad B and Chelsea asking for her dad. I was glad I was through with all that, even though I had been persuaded to take leave without pay for the year instead of resigning. There was so much else to do with life instead of sitting at a secretary's desk, handling computer and telephone all day. Which is what I was doing here, but, heh, it was my own stories I was typing. Except for writer's block and overnight guests and parties ... Once this party was over, back to Chikkamma: what made her stop living with him? If I could just crack that mystery, my story could get somewhere.

As I stopped for a light, I realized I was not alone. So used to being on my own, I had quite forgotten Kitu, but he didn't seem to mind. I told him that I hoped he could teach Iyer all about cooking in a Canadian kitchen. Kitu was excited: "Wowee, Iyer Uncle and he would cook up a storm, wowee." Neither of us knew how long Sam intended to stay, and I sure hoped it was not going to be long, but I didn't want to dampen Kitu's enthusiasm. However, it would be nice to get Iyer to cook for the next party. There was the South Indian part of our social orbit to whom we still owed a dinner. That would be heaven, indeed, to have someone else do the cooking. One of the main reasons I wanted to go back to Madras was to be able to escape kitchen work. I wanted to go back while servants were still available: the species would soon be phased out, I could see. Each successive visit showed their slow disappearance from houses which had had a fleet of domestics for generations. The working class preferred now to work in factories or hotels: the wages families could afford to pay could not possibly match what could be made at hotels or even sweeping the streets.

I was hellbent on sticking to my standard menu. But Kitu had his wish. And Iyer too. The next morning, I had one of those freak accidents that one is embarrassed to talk about because it makes one look such a klutz. I sprained my arm at the shoulder while washing my hair. I slipped in the tub, held on to the side-bar to check my fall but as I swivelled, instead of letting go of the bar, I held on and my arm turned. I screamed. Kitu came bounding up the stairs. I limped out, having got into my robe with great difficulty. Siv and Sam had already left, of course.

He helped me into my room, and then started laughing. "Amma, sweet amma," how lovely the endearment sounded! "You still have soap in your hair. Let me wash it out for you." And he did. And he promptly cleaned the washbasin and mopped up the bathroom floor. Then he made me lie down and massaged my arm. Click, he rotated something in my shoulder into position.

"When did you learn all this," I asked, marvelling at his dexterity, his masseur-touch.

"We are taught the art of massaging very early. We do get a thorough training, amma, three-four years."

"You mean, you ..." I stopped. The only thing I could think of was too mind-boggling.

"Yes, amma sweet amma," he said softly.

So that was his other family, the people who had trained him to be what he was. I needed time to digest the information.

"I'll rest for just a little while, Kitu, and then we have lots of work to do." He went away.

The massaging felt good, so good. But what he had said was sad, so sad. Girls, I had always thought of only girls. There are boy children too. No, I couldn't think about it. There was too much work to be done. I must have been crazy to invite fifty guests. I had better get up. But I needed a little more time. Kitu, poor Kitu, what a childhood! Yet he seemed happy. Sami was gentle and kind and loving. Yes, I had to agree I suppose, that Kitu was lucky.

I got dressed and went down. My arm seemed to have come back. But when I lifted the skillet off the counter to put it away, I almost dropped it. The twinge in my upper arm was torturous. Kitu was by my side in a trice.

"What am I going to do?" I moaned.

"Never fear, Kitu is here," he said. "Amma sweet amma," he chortled, "now I can make my *aviyal* for the party ! Now you can just sit and watch the way I said you should. Now Iyer Uncle and I will cook up a storm. What is his number?"

I called Sara. I told her I would be really really grateful if Mr. Iyer could come down for the day. I didn't know what I could or should tell her. When Iyer came to the phone, I explained what had happened. He too was openly delighted, though he did say how sorry he was to hear about my arm et cetera et cetera. I got Sara back on the phone and asked that Iyer take a cab since I couldn't drive. I made a mental note that I should ask him just what I could or could not tell Sara. His son might not take kindly to the idea of his father working as a cook. Some people were still touchy about what they thought were menial jobs, even after years in this country.

I waited outside with cash in hand for the cab, but it was Sara who brought him. I invited her in. She seemed rather tempted, I could see, but she declined. Some other time I would have to bridge the distance, I said to myself, some other time, once this party was over.

"You didn't get rid of it," Iyer said, as we walked in. "Now it is only the arm. No harm done, don't worry. But don't keep it too long. Some cancers, colon cancer for one, are dormant for ten years and then once they flare up ..." he didn't have to complete his thought, and he knew it.

We went over the new menu, for neither of them knew or cared about the north Indian meal I had planned. While Kitu was getting the rice cooker ready, I spoke to Mr Iyer. "Tell me, what do you know about Gayatri power — that one hundred thousand Gayatris will have some astounding result?" He laughed.

"You mean you don't believe that?" I was rather upset. Here he was, rushing to place the first pot on the stove before ten-thirty, which was Rahu's starting time today, but laughing away the power of the Gayatri, that I had already seen, or had I?

"I don't know, amma," he said, "All I know is that behind every prescribed ritual is the intent that we lead moral lives. We are told to salute the dawn because it is a good habit to start the day early. I don't see how repeating a mantra one lakh times will put the food on the table, and I am sure it is a man's moral responsibility to put food on the table."

"But food is not the be-all and end-all of life."

"That is what we Brahmins keep saying, even as we have our three square meals a day. But that is because we don't pay attention to what we pray for. When we change the sacred thread every August," he said, "we ask God to forgive us for our wrong actions, and we list them because God doesn't like giving blank cheques. One, on the list is, for the sin of being preoccupied with books when I should be working in the fields, please Lord, forgive me. Clear, isn't it? That even preoccupation with knowledge is not to be taken as above working in the fields to put food on the table? Speaking of which, I think Kitu is ready for us."

Siv should talk to Iyer, I thought. One hundred thousand Gayatris, bah. I would have to process later, I thought, what the basic contradictions in Iyer's statements and actions were. But one thing was definitely nice about him. Sometime in the afternoon, he came for a coffee break to where I was sitting, and in the course of conversation said that Kitu was a sweet child, even if fate had made him different outside from what he was inside. Yes, I liked a lot of things about Mr. Iyer, especially the way he called Sara and Kitu sweet children. But his paranormal powers did bother me.

In the late afternoon, when everything was cooked and the exhaust fan had whisked away all cooking odours so that only pleasant aromas emanated from the oven on simmer, Kitu and Iyer sat at the kitchen table drinking coffee. I was having my tea.

"So, will you be wearing your Mondetta T-shirt today?" I asked Kitu.

"Oh no, that is for a special occasion."

"Isn't today special enough?"

"Oh." He seemed nonplussed. "You don't want me out there, do you?"

"But of course, both of you."

Iyer said, "Oh no, I haven't brought a change of shirt or anything."

I insisted. From Siv's closet, I drew out a couple of Indian shirts of khadi cotton, and brought them down. One of them would have to do, I said. And I told Kitu to use his room but to come down for sure by six o'clock.

"I was thinking Iyer Uncle and I could play *pallankuzhi*," Kitu said a tad disappointed.

Iyer was enthusiastic. "You mean you have the shells and board? We could play for a little while." Again, they had become teenagers, almost with a teenager's cracking voice I swear.

"Of course, I carry them everywhere. Sami plays to please me but his heart isn't in it. And I have Ludo too. It is called Parcheesi here."

"With Snakes and Ladders on the other side?"

"No, two different boards. I bought them in New York."

"With the biggest snake going from 98 to 9?"

"Yes, but the tail is on 98 and the head on 9."

"That is illogical. Why is it like that? If you land on 98, the snake gobbles you up and you go to its tail. How can anyone have the head down?"

Illogical? I laughed to myself. What role did logic have in Iyer's world view? What could it have? A man who thought we were sitting on dynamite because of a geometric design copied from an old book. But then the old unease came over me. He had divined water where three professionals had failed. He had found his way to the exact spot where the brown envelope had been. Some other time, not now, I had to mull over these contradictions.

Seven

The evening was crowded. That I remember. The food was superb. Everyone who was there would remember that. The conversation? I am not so sure, though I was flitting from group to group all the time. And the ending of the evening?

The first guests came in at six-twenty. By six-forty there were thirty-five. By seven all had arrived, and then some. Stella, the music critic from *The Ottawa Citizen,* had phoned me in the afternoon saying she would like to meet Sam, and she now came with three others from the Music Department at Carleton. I must have told her to bring whoever else she thought might be interested in Sam's work. My old friend, Alice, had brought a young man newly arrived from India. There were a few of Siv's students who had not been on the guest list, but they were always welcome. If there were others, I didn't meet them.

With more people than we could thread our way through, Siv announced that there would be no formalities, not even the traditional one of Siv mixing the first drink for each guest. Each could decide when to eat, what to drink, to whom they wanted to introduce themselves.

It was good in a way that there were so many people. It absolved me of the task of hosting: I could just greet Ukkal and slip away; I could spend some time with Stella, whose columns had always intrigued me; generally I could keep an eye on the flow of food and conversation without being obvious. I had made sure that Haveli's would send a double order of everything — an extra ten or fifteen air miles on my MasterCard.

For the first couple of hours everything seemed to flow smoothly, and I was in control. For example, from the way Matthew was eyeing Kitu, I knew I'd better keep note of him from time to time. Matthew is one of my artsy friends, as Siv says; he means artsy-fartsy, but Siv doesn't use slang. Matthew runs a bookstore in a place just outside the Market, and has some rather interesting craft workshops. Almost everyone who saw Kitu was taken up with him but I knew Matthew's look. And I didn't know if Kitu would know how to cope with him. If Kitu could be so pleased with a Mondetta shirt, who knows how vulnerable he was to what Matthew had to offer, or take. A couple of times, I diplomatically steered Kitu into one or other of the predominantly women's circles.

Teresa, one of Siv's research assistants was in the same boat as Kitu. I had seen Harya, another of Siv's colleagues, making overtures at the last party, but Teri was not my business whereas Kitu was. As I weaved in and out of groups, I innocently asked Jennifer, who just happened to be standing next to Harya, for her opinion of Jane Gallop's recent book that argued she was all the better for having slept with her professors, male and female, in her graduate years, and with her students now that she was a senior professor herself. I slipped away, letting the chips fall where they will. I knew Karen, who was in the group at the time, would have a lot to say about the book.

And then there was Prof. Richards, whose first name is Ebenezer, so we tended to call him Prof. Richards. He is writing a history of the National Research Council, and tends to bore people out of their wits. He begins with the year 1916, when what became the NRC was started, and chronologically plods through the landmarks (what he considers landmarks are, unfortunately, just a series of dates and data) to whomever happens to meander within hearing distance. My standard rescue operation is to join him and lead him away with an "I'd like you to meet someone who'd love to hear about your work."

In every party, there are ego-talkers and there are passive listeners. Put two passive listeners together and you kill a party, for them anyway: put two ego-talkers together, and they will take care of themselves by leaving for more conducive pastures. The first time I did it this evening was when Prof. Richards was regurgitating data about the Tory years — how in 1923 Henry Marshall Tory, at age sixty, set about getting the best brains of the country to Ottawa, and by 1935, when he left office, he had accomplished his goal — and Prof. Richards went on to list the names and credentials and date of appointment of every scientist Tory had brought to NRC. I steered him away, much to the relief of his captives, to Sam, another ego-talker, except that his field is so much more interesting.

The second time I forayed to the rescue, Prof. Richards had come up to the 1940s. But this time I found myself quite fascinated with what he was recounting — the Habakkuk project, named after an Old Testament prophet. "Thou didst walk through the sea with thine horses, through the heap of great waters." The idea was to tow icebergs from the Arctic, and construct floating islands of ice in the North Atlantic, each weighing two million tons, that would act as an airstrip two thousand feet long by three hundred feet wide by one to two hundred feet deep, on these islands the warplanes could land, fuel, take off and bomb enemy territory. Lord Mountbatten apparently announced the project dramatically, "Gentlemen, I have here the means of winning the war." Churchill wouldn't let go of the idea even after it was shown that to cut a lozenge of ice that huge was not practical, and anyway would take much longer than the year he was prepared to give the scientists. I stopped and listened, and I think all of us were duly impressed, except for Joanne, who jumped in with "Maru, add this to your list of the m.m. syndrome. Even Mountbatten, who would have thought, even him!" And of course others wanted to know what the m.m. syndrome was, so Joanne explained. I don't think Prof Richards heard her — he is a little hard of hearing, or maybe he did but pretended not to. Anyway he ambled off in search of someone else so he could continue playing his phonograph record. The group reformed to discuss the m.m. syndrome with Joanne leading the debate. I would have loved to stay there but I had my hosting duties.

I went to say hello to my friend Adam, one of Siv's research assistants. He has a talent for imitating accents, and I had a new story I wanted to share with him. I made sure I greeted everyone in the group before addressing Adam with, "Adam I have a great story for you which I heard from Andrew Salkey at Harbourfront," and went on to tell it. Salkey was visiting one of the Caribbean islands, walking along the beach, when an idea for a short story came to him, a story of an old man who spent hours looking towards Africa — the story would be about him and his grandson. Wanting a typical island name for the boy, he went up to a group of fishermen and asked what name was the most common around the island. "In these here parts," said a fisherman, "Afa is a popular name." And so Salkey named him Afa, and a reviewer raved about the resonance of Africa in Afa, and Salkey himself was pleased at the serendipitous choice. Next time he visited the island, he showed the story to the fisherman who had given him the name and thanked him. The fisherman ran his eyes over the story, and said, "Am glad for you, man, but in these here parts we spell it Afa — A R T H U R."

Everyone duly laughed at my story, except Sandy from Nigeria. Adam, in an aside, told me that it had been bad timing, since Sandy had just ended a lecture on how white Canadians were so intolerant of African and Chinese accents but never complained about the incomprehensible British and Southern accents. Adam had tried to lighten him up with the old Shaw quip about Britain and the U.S.A. being separated by the Atlantic and the English language, but Sandy was not to be appeased. And then I had to butt in. "You win some, you lose some. It is that kind of an evening," I told Adam.

Sam was holding forth on his treatise about the import of the violin into Carnatic music. Alice was regaling her group with how the tuberculosis serum was injected in her day with sixty little stabs in the small of the back; how they had to line up, on one side of the curtain while the doctor went jab jab, jab, "Next," as though the nurses — of whom she was one — were a herd of cattle; how one of her friends went in with her corset on, you know those rubber corsets (and she laughed so much she had to pause) and the doctor had to pull it off her and the time he had of it ...

In short, it seemed that the evening was going really well. But then the clock struck twelve, if you know what I mean, and the carriage started turning into a pumpkin, not all at once but with steady acceleration.

I can swear we did not have more than the usual amount of drinks per guest at the bar. Siv has a formula based on statistics he has drawn up as to how many bottles of whiskey, vodka, beer, wine etc. would be needed, given the usual drinking habits of average drinkers. Our social circle had only average drinkers. If, by chance, someone turned out to be otherwise, we never invited him again. It has always worked, and Siv can tell you the ratio of beer drinkers to hard liquor drinkers in our usual crowd, and the ratio preference of white to red wine. Much earlier than usual, it seemed, many had imbibed more than seemed good for them. Yet the bottles were emptying only at the projected rate. And the food was disappearing at such a rapid pace, it couldn't be that anyone was drinking on an empty stomach. But something was happening. I looked for Siv but he was not to be seen.

First there were little verbal explosions here and there.

One group was discussing the Conawapa project and political skulduggery; Jagjit said, "So Ontario promises to buy power, Manitoba invests millions of dollars, and then Ontario shuts down its nuclear plants." Sanjay shouted, "Don't be so paranoid about inconsequentialities, you numbskull. Think about the more imminent possibility of nuclear waste getting into the water supply and then where would we be?"

Matthew and Sam were at each other, clearly a joust over Kitu, but ostensibly it was about the genealogy of the violin family of instruments.

Sandy's wife had a bigger chip on her shoulder than Sandy, and there were raised voices in her corner as she harangued over degrees of racism. Joanne's friend Andy got into a kerfuffle over political correctness and vigilantism. And John, I think it was John, was hotly arguing that with such emasculated governments, we just had no choice but to be vigilantes. The air was getting hot, no doubt about it.

On the spur of the moment, I started a game: passing around a sheet of paper, I told them to write their age and sex, no name or identifying sign, just their age and sex. There were nine men aged fifty-four; and the average age of the men in the room was 53.8. I sent another sheet around, yes or no to belief in there being a scientific basis to paranormal phenomena. The sheet did not come back. Instead, many started discussing the wording of the question, and definitions of the term. The room became hotter, and more windows were opened.

The young man newly arrived from India who had come with Alice came to life at this point. He had a lot to say about the power of the Baba who conjured Seiko watches from the air. "From up his sleeve more likely," said one of the cynics. "Baba's robe has sleeves so wide he could hide the Royal Mint up it." Kitu joined the group when voices got raised about sorcery and godmen. He narrated several stories about "kuttichatan" as they are called in Kerala. He bore first-hand testimony of men you could hire to harass anyone against whom you had a grudge: they conjured up kuttichatans who could make scorpions fall from the ceilings of even houses built with cement concrete; who could make one delirious even without touching them; who could give itches and headaches — all they needed was something that had touched the person you wanted punished, usually a piece of clothing, even a strip of clothing would do. Amanda added similar stories of voodoo dolls. The air was getting hotter. I looked for Siv. Maybe we could get some of the table fans from the basement. Anyway he was nowhere to be found.

My written question had set off several groups on topics related to paranormal and cult activities. It is amazing how much people know and remember about topics that interest them, and how well they marshall out facts and figures. Jonestown, Waco, Solar Temple, Heaven's Gate, as each topic came up, specialized groups reformed, and the room became hotter. More windows were opened. Since it had started raining soon after the party had started, the party couldn't spill over onto the patio or lawn.

Iyer was in a group that had started with the Solar Temple and gone on to comet insanity. Iyer took over and talked about eight-planet configurations and records of how they had affected civilizations, and gave his reason why on the basis of the planetary positions described in the *Mahabharata,* the battle of Kurukshetra could be placed exactly in the year 1538 BC He would have gone on to give chapter and verse from the epic to prove his point but he did not have Prof. Richards' ability to drone on. The moment he stopped to look up a reference in his head, someone started on Velikovsky's *Worlds in Collision* and battlelines were drawn in no uncertain terms.

In another part of the room, Sam loudly proclaimed, "Anyone with a shred of intelligence would see that there were patterns in history, that the hour brought forth the man, that great minds came in clusters in order to change the course of history — the musical trinity of Tyagaraja, Syama Sastri and Dikshitar were all born within miles of each other within the same decade. Handel and Bach were born in the same year, again just a few miles apart. The founders of three major religions, Confucius, Mahavir and Buddha, were all born within two decades of each other. Heinrich Schutz, Johann Schein and Samuel Scheidt were all born between 1825 and 1827. Surely this said something."

"All it says is that great minds, like other human beings, live and die," Matthew said, "unless of course some halfwit wanted to say that musicians are not mere human beings." At which Sam gave Matthew a resounding blow on the back of his head.

At exactly the same moment, Prof. Richards, who was now expatiating on the controversy in the 1950s over bringing the NRC under the Civil Service Commission, was knocked down by an assailant whom no one really saw in the act even though everyone heard someone shouting "Death to the Civil Service."

Stella's group, that had been discussing the pitch alphabet of the Greater Perfect system and how diatonic nomenclature had led to ambiguities of the chromatic scale, had gone back to the fundamentals of chromatic harmony in Renaissance Italy. The discussion broke up in chaos when Colin claimed he was an incarnation of Don Carlo Gesualdo and Stella was a goat.

Siv's senior colleague, Abe Miller, a greatly respected scientist, was continuing a thread that Siv had started about late recognitions — Wegener's plate tectonics and Chandrasekhar's black hole that he had told me about. Abe had talked about how Michael Polanyi was ignored from 1916 to the Fifties, how Peter Mitchell was ignored from the Fifties to the late-Seventies, and now Abe had come to Barbara McClintock, who was ignored for forty years before she got the Nobel Prize in 1983. At this point, Karen, who always gets steamed up about the way women have been ignored in science put in her bit about Carolyn Herschel and Rosalind Franklin, and then threw herself at Abe, felling both of them to the floor. This was so unlike Karen, I knew something infernal was going on. Matthew, Sam, Andy, Colin, yes, it could be jealousy, fanaticism, drink ... But Karen throwing Abe to the floor at the very moment that someone shouted, "Death to the Civil Service," and knocked down Prof. Richards!

Priti, dear to me for herself and for being the daughter of my old friends the Moghes, had started the evening talking about her medical internship, but was now moderating a heated discussion about Princess

Di. There again, opinion was sharply divided: was she a cancer that would eat up the Windsors? Was she a role model for the Twenty-First Century? Was all this hype about her charity work a show put on by her and the organizations behind the causes? What a bounder that baldy was, and to think he would be king one of these days ... At which Bea, who I guess had the Daughters of the Empire in her blood unbeknownst to us, shouted, "The paparazzi and royalty vilifiers like you and you and you," as she swung her handbag at each, "are going to be poor Princess Di's death one of these days." Bea was one of those unfortunates with kleptomaniac tendencies, and she had stuffed into her handbag a marble bookend I had picked up years ago in Teotihuacan: it swished around like a veritable Vishnu Chakra, felling several people to the ground.

In a matter of minutes, the house was in total chaos. Some fled upstairs, and huddled on the steps, keeping their distance from the berserk core of activity downstairs. But even on the stairway, someone intentionally or accidentally kicked the one on the step below and the domino effect brought several more people to the floor.

Mr. Iyer was picking his way through the crowd towards me. "Where is it?" he said, "Get it at once. Get Kitu to dig a pit and bury it for now in the backyard."

And in all this chaos, Siv was still nowhere to be seen. It was too much. How could he be so irresponsible? At every turn every day for years he had left me to manage everything that he dumped quite unceremoniously on me — social engagements at short notice; running the house; chauffeuring children from one class to another; all the repairs involving plumber, electrician, handyman; bills, contractors, everything; all with a cheerful "Behind every successful man is a good secretary," but this was just too much. Leaving me with this mayhem.

Unless, oh my god, he isn't that irresponsible, which means ... a stroke, a heart attack ... I rushed upstairs, tripping over people who sat on the steps in the red alert position that air-hostesses tell us to take, head on knees, arms around knees. Iyer followed me closely, and I could hear him take the monkey position, head down, knees bent, snout thrust forward. "First get it," he panted. "First I have to find Siv," I said. Occasionally, at these parties, Siv would slip away to his study to get his head back together, as he said. But he'd never been away for more than a few minutes. I hadn't seen him in the last half hour or more, though I had looked for him often enough. The keys to all the rooms were kept in the bathroom, in the cabinet under the washbasin.

What a stupid place, I realized for the first time, as I waited for whoever was inside to come out. We had two washrooms off the living room, but of course that wasn't enough for this evening.

"Come. Look at this," Iyer called to me but I refused to heed him. I took the keys and opened the study. Siv was not in his study.

"Come, come, come, come," Iyer whispered hoarsely, holding open the door to my den. It looked like a tornado had passed through it. All the cartons were upside down, papers strewn around, and there on the ceiling was the Sri Chakra. Have you ever seen the face of a person from the head of the bed? Try it, it is a scary sight, with the eyes where the mouth should be. And when the eyes look upwards at you, ugh, it is scary all right. So also with the Sri Chakra, only a thousand times worse. When seen from above or from the front, it is a geometric design, awesome in its symmetry, beautiful in its lines and curves. But see it from below and it is a face, the face of Goddess Kali on the warpath, red eyes, lolling tongue, hair outspread, spear held against the cheek ready to be hurled.

"Get it," Iyer panted, "Get it before it flies out the window."

"I have to find Siv," I said, clutching the key to the bedroom.

"Get it first."

"The window is closed. It can't fly out. Siv first."

"What is a closed window to something that can do this to a room? Get it before it kills Sivaraman," he said.

That threw me. I started scrambling for a chair to reach the painting. Then good sense returned. This man was insane. A piece of paper with a design on it, for godssake, what was I thinking? Every minute counts in a stroke or heart attack. One can reverse the effects of a heart attack completely if one got something, what is its name, into the patient within half an hour. I rushed into the bedroom. I could see Siv's back. He was sitting on the carpet, facing the window. He must have fallen, I thought, rushing towards him. Iyer pulled me back. "Sh," he said. "Wait."

"Louder," Iyer said. "Louder." He quickly sat where he was, cross-legged, facing the window, facing east I realized. The sound of the mantra from Siv joined Iyer's.

"Om bhur bhuvah svaha ..." followed by twenty-four syllables, the words a simple salutation to the Prime Effulgence, but concentrate on the sound and meaning together and it is the music of the spheres, holding the universe in harmony. Not to be broadcast but whispered into the initiate's ears, who promises by all that is sacred to keep it in trust. The Gayatri.

I came out and closed the door softly behind me. I went to my room and waited. Soon, the Sri Chakra floated down from the ceiling and lay on the ground, just a harmless square of parchment paper with a geometric design within a circle. Iyer and Siv came out of the room, and went downstairs without saying a word.

The guests continued just where they had left off twenty minutes ago, except that they would not remember the break in the continuum, the madness of those twenty minutes. They would remember how some tempers had frayed and voices had been raised, and how opening all the windows had cooled hotheads so they could go back to the table still laden with so much scrumptious South Indian food and desserts that made many of them decide that if Iyer ever opened a South Indian restaurant, they would altogether stop cooking at home on Saturdays.

*****

Next morning, Siv and I sat at our morning coffee, he doing the morning crossword.

"Say something," I said, "Speak to me."

He put the newspaper down, and looked at me over his reading glasses. "Interesting evening," he said. "Makes me think I should start over again and do it more scientifically, though keeping a minute-by-minute record of electromagnetic fields of the brain and the environment might be a little onerous. I don't suppose the NRC would care to fund it," he stroked his chin.

"You are not serious?"

"The Parapsychological Association might be interested. Maybe the people who worked with Jahn and Dunne at Princeton could be persuaded to come up with funds, let me see who else, there is Honorton's group in Edinburgh ..."

"Stop," I said, "Stop it. You are not going to do any such thing."

"On the other hand, that music ensemble, is it Maharishi Mahesh Yogi's? What is it called, "Celestial Music" or something? Yes, "Gandharva Music," have already been doing a lot of work on reducing crime in major cities by generating a concentrated force field of simultaneous meditation ..."

"Stop or I'll scream," I said.

"There was enough of that last evening. By the way, Maroo my Maroo, you kept your cool, I am proud of you."

"Don't try to hedge. Flattery won't get you anywhere."

"Sh, don't shout. Poor Sam is still sleeping. The boy did a good job yesterday; he and Iyer, fantastic. Sam seems overly protective of the boy, don't you think?"

"He takes very good care of Kitu, and the boy is happy."

Siv picked up the defensiveness in my voice. "You mean he is, they are ... I'll be darned."

"You are not going to work on this mumbo jumbo," I said. "You are not. You are going to finish your stint at NRC, and we are going back to Manipeg. I much prefer *that* m.m. syndrome to this. *That* is clear, comprehensible, normal, but this I can't take. No way."

"Maybe you are right, Maroo my Maroo. As I said, one Velikovsky per century is enough. But who knows, after all the next century isn't that far off."

Darkest Before Dawn

Jayant put away his violin. He couldn't get the right note. He wasn't surprised. Everything he touched turned to dust and ashes. Treachery had been his companion as far back as he could remember. Everyone to whom he felt close ended up betraying him. He should be used to it by now; yet each time he was caught unprepared, each time it was a sudden rapier thrust. No, that was too dramatic, too romantic an image, only Romeos and Cæsars got hit that way ... There was this commercial fishhook, a fail-proof hook that twisted itself ninety degrees into the fish, and the fish died a long slow death.

His sister's eyes had twisted the hook into him. It had started off with her trying to tell him how much they'd miss him but all too soon it reached a point when she coldly said, "I am glad you are pitching out because that is the only way you'll get into that thick skull of yours that we are different, and no matter what we do, we are never going to fit in here. Take to the road, get high, sleep around, but still and all, we'll never belong except in our own homes."

"Fuck off, Jyo, you'll see."

"All those expletives. All the 'in' jargon. But you are never going to be one of the boys. Not that I see why anyone would want to fit into this mould."

"Don't you come at me with all that crap about morals and Hindu values. I've had an earful from Dad for nineteen fucking years. He and his pipe dreams about India. Why the hell didn't he stay there? A nuclear scientist, Trombay, the whole bit. He'd have been somebody by now. Instead he quits the place to be and rots here selling houses." Jayant picked up a table tennis ball and squeezed it in the palm of his left hand. As he raised his hand to run it through his hair, a habit he had, a faint smell of camphor from the ball wafted up, arousing deep nebulous memories of another place another time.

Jyoti said, "It couldn't have been easy for him to pack up everything and move out at thirty-five. And it is no bed of roses here, mowing the lawn, painting the house, and a hundred menial chores which were done by servants in the luxury of his ancestral home."

"Some house that, a sprawling shambles handed down untouched from the time of the Peshwas where you have to walk half a mile to get to the shithouse, Jeesus. And the irony is that all that crap about giving his kids a better future was just a way of rationalizing his failure."

"Stop that, Jay, stop it."

"And you know what your trouble is, kid? You are on the moon with that Pierre of yours, holding hands and singing moonshine into his blonde hair. If you'd get laid a couple of times you'd come off all those preachy echoes of Dad's slogans."

He looked at her, and there was something in her eyes that drew him sharply against the wall of recognition. In a whisper he said, "You haven't, sis, you haven't?" It was clear Jyoti had.

Jayant grabbed the darts from the table and zinged them at the board in lightning sequence. All three lodged in the inner circle, one dead centre.

Jyoti had slung her denim jacket over her shoulder, and gone to the stairs, leaving Jayant amid his open suitcase and stacked T-shirts.

*****

Jyoti went to her room and her fingers trembled as she tried in vain to shut the door on her memory.

They were in India still at the time. She was about ten. Jayant, whose school, even though run by the same Roman Catholic Mission as hers, had a longer December vacation so he was visiting cousins in Delhi. In an interclass recitation competition, Jyoti had been chosen to represent her section. She was already known for her talent for memorizing poems overnight and this was not the first time she had competed. That evening, as she memorized the selected poem, the import of the lines hit her:

> Oh call my brother back to me!
> I cannot play alone:
> The summer comes with flowers and bee,
> Where is my brother gone?

She burst into tears. The scenes were so clear — Jayant run over by a lorry; Jayant on the Yamuna, his usually curly hair straightened out and streaming behind him as he floated feet first; Jayant tripping on the railway track and being scooped up and flung away by the engine's cow-catcher. Jyoti cried herself to sleep, sure Jayant was dead. She went to school next day, her stomach knotted with cramps. But she couldn't withdraw for that would be letting down her team. And so she sing-songed her way — ti dum ti dum ti dum ti da — that way the meaning didn't matter.

*****

Jayant picked up the violin and ran his bow lightly across the strings. He tried an old melody, the very first he had learned. And he remembered.

He remembered his grandmother, seated in the courtyard of their ancestral house on the familiar thick woven mat of silk straw.

The courtyard was large and rectangular and seemed cut in two halves. The far half had trees, a bakul tree that spread its branches over the far right wall, and there were flowering bushes of jasmine and raat-ki-rani, and a clump of banana trees.

Along the far left wall was the vegetable patch from which the gardener brought in coriander leaves or mint and fresh okra or long beans every morning. In the middle of the far wall was a door beyond which were latrines and still farther the servants' quarters. The nearer half of the courtyard was flanked by the house on one side, by storerooms and bathrooms on another and by the kitchen and dining room on the third. Here, the ground had been plastered smooth with years of daily sprinkling of cow-dung water so that it was an even mellow yellow, hard as a tennis court. At the centre was a planter of whitewashed brick for the tulsi plant, complete with little niches where the clay lamps and incense sticks could burn despite rain. And near it, under the shade of a parijata tree sat his grandmother with her violin.

It was a scene etched in Jayant's memory, a scene to which his spirit returned in quiet moments, a scene which he sought out when storms came up. A scene where everything was in place, exactly in place. Aji playing her violin every day just after her three o'clock tea.

At the time of his first visit back to his grandparents from Canada, Jayant had been fourteen. Not young enough to admit openly that he wanted to sit by his grandmother, nor old enough to take the initiative and speak to her. He was self-conscious of his Marathi: it had rusted in the last four years away from India. Even though his parents spoke Marathi at home, he and Jyoti had switched to English and his kid brother, Krish, could not even understand Marathi. Jayant could not bring himself to enunciate once familiar words lest he made a fool of himself. So he lingered every afternoon, on the charpai or the swing, a book in hand, close enough to smell the potpourri that gave all the contents of her mahogany chest of drawers a subtle jasmine fragrance, but not letting on that he was listening.

Sometimes Aji sang as she played: she had a well-trained voice. Even his untrained ears discerned the felicity with which her voice moved like rippling water through the notes, the way she manoeuvred her voice in the alapanas like water falling over rocks in shallow rapids.

One day, as he sat on the swing biting into a green guava and pretending to read, she stopped playing after just a few minutes. He waited without turning his head, disappointed.

"Jayant."

"Yes, Aji."

"Come here. I've never heard you sing, baba."

He came over, lay on his stomach and raised himself, his elbows just inside the edge of her mat, cupping his face in his hands. "Aji, I don't know any good songs."

"Come, come, you know many English songs, right?"

"Oh, I'll never sing those. They sound so awful compared to yours." He laughed, embarrassed.

"When some say that, I know they just need some persuasion, but when others say it, I know they mean it."

"And which am I, Aji?" he said teasingly, holding out two fingers. She clasped both and then took his hands between hers.

"Why, Jai baba, your palms are calloused. What have you been doing in Canada? Are you a woodcutter there?" She too knew how to tease.

"Aji, even woodcutters there have Palmolive soft hands," he hummed the tv commercial tune. "We have machinery for everything." He imitated the sound and action of a chainsaw and then proudly said, "I got all these here, from chopping wood. Ask Chhotu."

Chhotu was an old retainer, well over sixty and still straight-backed and steady armed. He chopped wood for the stove on which bathwater was warmed for the whole family. Chhotu had gone into a tizzy when the vialyati baba (the boy from foreign lands) had first wanted to chop wood but Jayant had cajoled him into yielding. Chhotu had taught him how, but only after absolving himself of responsibility by calling on all the gods to bear witness to the stubbornness of the young master. Some of the callouses were due to tree-climbing, an old pastime that Jayant had picked up with alacrity within days of coming to Pune.

"Do you know where I would like your callouses to be? here, and here and here," she touched the inner tips of the fingers of his left hand, "like mine." She ran his fingers over hers and he could feel them just under the fine pale brown skin.

"When Savitri wrote to me years ago that you were taking piano lessons, I told myself I would teach you to play the violin and leave my violin for you."

Jayant's eyes smiled brilliantly as he leaned forward. "Would you, really?" and then because he had meant the bequest, he added quickly, "Teach me, I mean?"

Aji laughed, her small white teeth circled by the red tinge of chunam that spiced the betel-leaf roll she ate after lunch. "It is quite all right to mean both, baba, and I really would love to do both, teach you now and leave the violin for you when it is time for me to go. Can you believe that no one in our family — little Anu is my forty-eighth descendant your Uncle Balwant tells me — not one has taken to the violin? We have vocalists, dancers, tabla and sitar players but no violinists. Not one."

"You have one, now," Jayant said, and in the next three months he had picked up the rudiments of classical music on the violin.

Aji died two years later. Had she left him her violin? Perhaps he would know only when his grandfather died.

His inheritance. Just outside old Pune, in the shadow of Shanwar Wada the stronghold of the Peshwas, within sight of the Hill of Lakshmi whose slopes housed their family deity Vithoba. His inheritance: trees that had stood there since the time a patriot had climbed the sheer face of the Moghul fortress with a rope tied to the tail of a giant lizard and earned for himself the name of Ghorpade; fields and villages that had increased gradually since the time Ram Shastri, to whom the family traced their lineage, had left Pune vowing never to return until the murder of Narayan Rao had been atoned with the ascension of Madhav Rao. Jayant remembered every detail of the proud family history that had been passed on to him through bedtime stories.

His inheritance. Foreclosed by his father.

How impatient his father had been to leave India! Jayant remembered the trips from Bombay to Delhi for their immigration formalities: the numerous trips to Pune to fill out forms for which only the family lawyer and munshi knew the details; what property had he inherited? what had he added? moveable, immoveable? income tax? arrears? did he have proof there were no arrears? had he resigned his job? had he proof his resignation had been accepted? did he owe his employers money? did he have proof he didn't? would he repatriate the money he'd spend on airline tickets?

Forms, legal advice, bribes just to get people to do what it was their job to do. In order to expedite the paperwork, his father had legally renounced all claim to ancestral and paternal property.

And now he was a real estate broker.

Betrayal, Jayant thought, his lifelong companion.

*****

Jyoti parked her car near the Khoslas' driveway, even though it was the no-parking side. Picking up her cousin Priti would take only a minute, she thought. Kamla, who was eight years old, same as Priti, opened the door after fumbling with the latch and key. She pushed the stool away as Jyoti entered, and Jyoti knew she was alone and had looked through the peephole before opening the door.

"Come in, didi, Mom just went out to pick up Dad. She'll be back in a minute."

"Everything is so quiet here. Where is Priti?"

"She never came. Didn't you know? Aunty Veejala phoned to say Priti couldn't come today but she promised she could sleep over the weekend. It's going to be so much fun." Kamla went on to tell Jyoti of the plans she had for the weekend.

So like Aunt Vee to have changed her plans and to forget to inform Jyoti.

"Please do stay, didi, and see my science project." Jyoti obligingly took off her boots and was about to follow the girl to her room when the doorbell rang. Both went to answer it.

"First check through the peephole," Kamla repeated the injunction that no doubt had been given to her a dozen times before her mother had left.

Jyoti opened the door. "Collecting," said one of the two boys at the door, ready to tear the yellow tab for the newspaper subscription."

"Nobody's home," Kamla said, "you'll have to come later."

"Nobody's home," the boy mimicked to his companion. "What you see ain't people but ghosts," and both laughed far more loudly than the joke warranted. Jyoti closed the storm door and was about to close the inner door when she heard the boys shout, “Paki, Paki house. Dirty, dirty.”

A shiver went down her spine. She wondered if she’d heard right. “What did they say?” she asked. Kamla nodded mutely.

“Did he say Paki?” Kamla nodded again.

Jyoti opened the door and walked out in her stockings. One of the boys had just thrown a snowball at the window, and the other was about to follow suit but stopped at seeing Jyoti and pretended to clean his gloves with the snow. Jyoti caught the newspaper boy by his coat collar and dragged him into the house.

“Did you say something?”

“Nothin’. I didn’ say nothin’,” he mumbled sullenly.

“I heard someone shout ‘Paki.’ It couldn’t have been you, could it?”

“Wasn’t us.”

“Now, who could it have been, do you think? eh?” He struggled to shake himself free. She unzipped his parka with her left hand so she could get a better hold of him. The other boy stood on the steps, wondering what to do. Jyoti shut the door, stood with her back to it, and turned the boy with both her hands so he had to face her. Then she let go of him.

“You want to grow up a barbarian, eh? This is a great country but snot-faced kids like you are stinking it up.”

She chucked him on his chin so he had to look at her. “We are getting a little tired of obnoxious pigs like you, and our older boys have formed a cleanup brigade. Did you know I have only to make a phone call to get them to take care of you? They might not move in today or tomorrow but you can bet on it they will move in on you when you are not looking. When they are done with you, even your mothers won’t recognize you, eh? And they’ll throw what remains of you in the garbage can in your backlane. You wouldn’t like that, would you?”

The boy stood as though she were still holding him.

She whipped out a colour clipping of a California quartet with trendy spiked hair and jackets. The picture had happened to be on the back of a newspaper item she had cut out for her Sociology term paper but she knew the quartet were just right for what she wanted now. She waved it in front of him. “Just to give you fair warning, this is them. How come you haven’t heard of them, eh?”

“Can I go, now?” he tried to sound nonchalant and failed.

"There's something you have to say, remember? Starts with an S and it is not your favourite four-letter word."

"I'm sorry," he said.

"Be sure to tell your friend, and anyone else you care to tell. And don't forget the garbage can. I should tell them the BFIs are easier. That's an idea." She pushed him out, closed the door and watched him through the window. She was trembling inside with a deep sense of power that frightened her.

Kamla was looking at her with her round eyes now rounder with admiration. "Oh, didi, did you look at his face? He was so scared he'd have peed in his pants if you'd let go."

Jyoti ran her fingers through the girl's hair absently.

Kamla wore her hair like most everyone her age, parted at the middle, feathered at the sides. She looked like every other eight-year-old, in blue jeans with an open-laced shoe on the hip pocket, a plaid shirt ... exactly like everyone her age, born here and unaware of any other place, leave alone any other country.

"Have you ever peed in your pants?" she asked.

Kamla laughed, "I've sometimes felt like, but of course never really done it. Oh no."

"When have you felt like that?"

"You know," (how like her kid brother Krish she used that phrase with the stress on "you", Jyoti thought,) "these junior highs who hang out at the Seven-Eleven — they make swear signs," she giggled with embarrassment.

"Do they call you Paki?"

"Not when I'm with Sandy and the rest. We always walk home together."

Jyoti felt nauseous. Her outburst had worked. It was frightening that Vithal, Priti's brother who was in the angry-young-man phase, should be right, oh god, she had acted exactly as her cousin would have them act, and it had worked. Or had it? Had she only jeopardized the poor girl's walks home?

Jyoti's stomach was all knotted up. It was her first encounter with racism. Oh, she had heard of incidents all right. With Vithal as cousin, there was no way she could have stayed ignorant, though she had thought he exaggerated everything. But now she had felt it for herself, the sudden uncontrollable spasm of fear and shock at hearing the word "Paki" flung at her.

It was just a matter of time, she told herself, before the problem resolved itself. Just wait a couple of generations and there'd be a lot more interracial kids. Her own for example. They would be beautiful; they always were, these children of two races. One just had to wait ... Jyoti caught herself short as other thoughts spilled over. Pierre, was he the man? But how could she doubt it, why this nagging fear? One thing at a time, she told herself, and the thing right now was to get her term papers and exams out of the way. She would not think of anything but the exams. Not about Vithal, not about Pierre. But how could she clear her mind of them, of those junior high boys she had never seen who made obscene and intimidating gestures to eight-year-old girls? What about Priti? Jyoti broke into a cold sweat. And what about Pierre? Was he the man? Would he ever understand what and how one feels when they have the word "Paki" flung at them?

*****

Jyoti's words had twisted the hook into him. Jayant felt he would gladly run his sword through Jyoti's boyfriend, Pierre. That guy was slimy. There was something altogether suspect about his appearance; something phony about his symmetrical face that looked like a plastic surgeon's cast of Adonis; his hair a perpetual Resdan commercial, greaseless, blow-dried, each hair bouncing back into place separately; his clothes that seemed taken out of glossy magazines. He earned good money though he was a college dropout, and he drove a Porsche. Except that he hadn't been driving lately. Jayant knew that his licence had been suspended for three months but didn't know just why ... did Jyoti know? Three months ago he would have asked Pierre the most personal questions without hesitation, but now he hated the guy so much he couldn't get past even the formalities of greeting. And at this moment he knew why — his instinct had alerted him to what Jyoti had just told him.

Betrayal. His life was haunted by shadows. Pierre whom he had loved was a guttersnipe.

Betrayal had been by his side always. Jayant strummed listlessly on the violin with his fingers. Yes, of course he was jealous of Pierre. Not jealous in the narrow textbook way that reduced everything to the physical and to complexes neatly pigeonholed with pretentious pseudo-scientific names. Jyoti was an extension of himself. It was a sacred inviolable bond that could be expressed only in symbols. Like the rakhi girls tied round their brothers' wrists on Rakshabandhan day; like the Rajput wedding rite where the bride's brother stood at the gate of the house and challenged the coming bridegroom to a symbolic duel, after which they embraced and went in together to the bride who waited with roses to garland the groom.

Jayant sipped at a pop that had gone flat. Some part of him was still resisting. Hogwash, it said, all this hype about rituals but another part knew it was not rituals he was talking about.

He had loved Pierre once, and not without cause. Therefore he should be able to love him again. Jyoti loved Pierre: and if she was not as radiant as she should be, it was because of them — he and Dad and Ma — their instinctive resistance to this alien seducer who had pulled away one of their own. They were taut like high-tension wires that vibrate almost unseen with sounds almost unheard.

The shadows around him, undefined but familiar, moved to some inaudible theme song of the collective unconscious of all their lives. Jayant placed the violin carefully beside him.

Like the headlights of cars that paused at the STOP sign across the street and cast on the living room wall distinct shadows of the leaves and fruit and branches of the ornamental crabapple tree below the large window, his memory, or need, from time to time shone on silent shadows within, defining one or two with recognizable outlines whereby they came alive with a face and a name — Ajoba's library, Aji's jasmine-scented saris, the STOP sign across the street, Jyoti's denim jacket, the smell of camphor in the niche of the tulsi tree, the ridiculous oversized billboards on Pembina Highway advertising Stanfield briefs and Cougar boots, all came together in an epiphany of vibrations.

He would do with due grace and honour what he had no doubt done with due grace and honour in a hundred past lives: when Pierre came on his white mare with plumed silk turban tasselled with red and white flowers, he would meet him with drawn sword; sheathing it, he would anoint Pierre with sacred vermilion and turmeric, and embrace him, with stars and moon and assembled guests as witness.

The dark night of the body was over.

How We Won Olympic Gold

Three stories stand out from the scores of events and experiences that made up my recent visit back home to India: how Bunto got toilet-trained; how I almost broke up two schoolchums' marriages and my own; and our winning Olympic gold.

I'll start with the last one first because that's the way I am. After a trip back, everything is topside down, there being such mountains of things — material and memory — and nothing gets put away because the moment one gets back, the waiting routine of rat-race chomps away at us thirty-two hours a day, and weekends fly by.

How we won the gold. You know your end of the story already but this is what happened at mine.

It is not that T. is a village far from civilization. Seat of maharajahs, it is a city all right, with its Central Avenue ending in the great big temple, its three palaces (all of which are now either government offices or tourist hotels) and cantonment and what have you.

But when it comes to telephone exchanges and long-distance calls, we are on another planet altogether. I should have realized it but when one is halfway around the world, one forgets that T. is not Delhi or Madras. So when the travel agent phoned to say that all flights were confirmed and I turned to Siv and asked should I really, really go, would he be all right? and he said, of course I should and of course he would be, and I made the mistake of saying, "Promise you'll phone me once in a while." He said he would phone me every Tuesday and Friday night and I said, that would be lovely. I'll live for Tuesdays and Fridays. You'd think he'd be flattered and give me a fond pat but what he said was, "Darn, don't get confused. It means Wednesday and Saturday mornings for you. And listen. I don't want to hear all about your day — what you bought and where you went or whom you met. I want to be told all about Bunto and nothing but. Write it down so you don't forget when I call: every new word he picks up, everything. And if he falls ill, for godssake keep me informed of everything. I mean it, abso. everything. Don't think to spare me the worry. Promise you won't hold back any details, promise?"

I heard that speech, with minor variations, about one hundred and forty-seven times between then and the time I walked through the security gates at Manipeg Airport with Bunto in my arms. Even though I often enough felt like hitting him over the head, I also felt sorry for him. That husband of mine loves his son, abso. dotes on him, and I felt awfully guilty about separating them for two months.

Those phone calls became a major exercise in timing and patience mainly because the telephone was three-doors away from ours, at Aunt Kamu's (no relation of ours, needless to say), and every Wednesday and Saturday morning became a large-scale production effort that involved many people.

Bunto and I reached my parents' house on a Tuesday morning. What with the overnight train journey and jet lag and friends and relatives dropping in to welcome Bunto, I forgot to tell anyone about the telephone-call arrangements for seven o'clock on Wednesdays and Saturdays.

Wednesday morning I was awakened by Mother. "It is a phone call," she said, in that ominous whisper we reserve for bad news. I jumped out of bed. "Is it seven o'clock already?" It was still dark outside. "No, hardly four, but hurry." I was about to lift the baby but she motioned me out of the room. Groggy with interrupted sleep, I did not register her worry and so didn't think to tell her it was a routine call and I followed the servant maid to Aunt Kamu's.

"Listen, woman!" Uncle Ramu was bellowing into the phone as I reached their front door. "No, I am not Maru but I want to speak to Siv, I mean Dr. Sivaraman," but clearly the operator was not to be shaken out of her procedural exactitude of how to handle person-to-person calls. I took the receiver, and on identifying myself, the call went through. Uncle Ramu, satisfied after the first thirty seconds that all was well with Siv and that the call was just part of a routine arrangement, stopped hovering protectively over me, and dismissed with a sweep of his hand the half dozen heads that had already converged at the door.

Siv was obviously practising what he had preached about preparing written notes before phoning. He marshalled out his questions, and wanted only one-word answers judging by the time he gave me between questions: Was the flight on time? Had there been enough milk or had they run out as usual the ... (four letter words)? Had his brother met us at Bombay Airport? Did customs give me a hassle about all those cartons of diapers and baby food? How was Bunto's stomach reacting to the change of water? Was I insisting on boiled water? Did I have mosquito netting for his bed? etc. etc.

When I could get in a question of my own, I asked why he was calling at this unearthly hour. Because Rita had invited him over for dinner and he wanted to check that we'd reached safely.

But why at four o' clock for godssake? Because sometimes it took forever to get the connections and, hell, the day starts early in India so why was I hollering? You've woken up the whole street, for godssake, and was it Rita or Neela? It was Neela and I should know it took close to an hour driving out there but geez he was sorry for calling so early but how could he enjoy Neela's famous samosas unless he knew for sure we'd reached okay, and did Bunto miss him? "Yes," I said, "Bunto missed him." And how about me, did I miss him? "Yes," I said, "but please don't call before five o'clock." "What?" he said, "What did you say?" "Yes," I shouted, "I missed him too, very very much, and would he take care?" "What?" he said, he couldn't hear me at all, "What?"

Just then, Pichai our servant maid came in, carrying Bunto who was howling his head off. Siv heard it, could have heard it even without the phone it seemed, and started shouting all uptight about his baby and would I please, please take good care of him, and I kept saying the baby was fine and he went on about boiled water and diaper rash and going easy on medication, until we suddenly got cut off.

Meanwhile, other heads had joined the cluster at the door, and my end of the conversation had been relayed along with creative reconstruction of Siv's side of the exchange. And the baby was still screaming because he was being passed from hand to hand: "The darling. Wasn't he exactly like his grandpa?" The gold nugget, what a voice he had!" "Ammamma, poor child, he misses his daddy."

"Did you hear how she misses him?" chuckle, chuckle. "Hardly a day since she's arrived and already," wink, wink. "That poor man, our Siv Ayya, left all alone." "Un unh, didn't you hear he's dining with some white woman, Rita's the name." "Wherever Rama lives should be Sita's Ayodhya," Aunt Kamu said, with a disapproving shake of her head, continuing the stance with which she had greeted me — about how it was bad enough that I'd had my baby in some heathen land but it was downright inauspicious that I should come without my husband on this my first visit after my first baby.

So that's what happened on the first Wednesday. Siv did not call me before six o'clock after that but all too often the call came through only after 10 o'clock, which meant that I had to spend half the morning hanging out at Uncle Ramu's under Aunt Kamu's colourful but crude tirade against the world at large. And, more disconcerting, half the community waited with me.

Just why they did is one of those inexplicable aspects of community living. On Wednesdays and Saturdays, the day's routine was paralysed for many of us in the lane until I'd got my telephone call. The vegetable vendor went so far as to take it as an omen: if I got it close to six o'clock, it would be a good day for her; if it did not come by seven, she had to break a coconut for special protection from the malignant fates that so loved to torture her.

I could tell you a story for every one of those Wednesdays and Saturdays (which mercifully changed to just Saturdays after my return from a visit to my in-laws) that I spent at my parents' house in T.

But the Olympic gold has been kept waiting in the wings too long. So let me get on with it.

It happened the day before I was to leave for Bombay and on to Manipeg: Saturday, September 24, 1988.

By now I had got into a routine. I left Bunto sleeping, in charge of Pichai, and started out for Uncle Ramu's. Pichai, as usual, was sweeping the front veranda and yard before sprinkling water and making the kolam design. I had the usual harangue with her about keeping within hearing distance, of Bunto, and washing her hands of all this dust before attending to him. She gave her usual lecture about how I had changed, all snooty and bossy using words no one could understand when all along she, and I, knew what a messy kid I had been, always falling into fresh cow dung (it had happened once, when I was four) and I wasn't any the worse for having been carried all the time in her unwashed arms, was I?

I did my usual chores while I waited. I cut vegetables for Aunt Kamu, and churned the cream into butter; I read aloud from the vernacular newspaper to Uncle Ramu's aunt who was now old and half blind, Bunto was brought over around 8 o'clock and I gave him his breakfast. 9 o'clock and still no phone call. I had dozens of packing details to attend to but I knew Siv well enough to know that if I did not confirm my travel plans with him, I would have to pay for his two day worry with two years of rebukes. There had been a slight change in my itinerary: our flight would reach Montreal two hours earlier than the one marked on the copy posted on our fridge door back in Manipeg, and I thought I would ask him to arrange a visit to Balwant's who lived close to Dorval. It would be nice to shower and relax so we could be fresh and dressed up when he received us back home.

It was about 9:45 when the phone rang. Instead of the usual questions about Bunto, Siv was roaring jubilantly and the words echoed and re-echoed against each other but I caught the contagion of his excitement even before I untangled his words, "WE'VE WON THE GOLD!"

I yelled back, "Fantastic! WE'VE WON OLYMPIC GOLD!"

The cry was picked up by Aunt Kamu's grandson, Nari, and spread quickly down the length of the lane, "We've won a gold."

Siv said, "Ben Johnson did it for us. 9:79 seconds! 9:79!"

"P.T. Usha's done it," someone shouted at the door, "I told you bad heel or no P.T. would go for it!"

"Usha, my foot. She shouldn't have been there in the first place. All that mumbo jumbo about not competing in the prelims. Usha's just a lame duck."

"O yeah?"

"Yah."

The slanderer and knight errant took their fists outdoors over P.T. Usha.

I waved NO, NO with my hand. "Not Usha?" Nari asked. No, I motioned, as Siv shouted on, "Carl Lewis was a whole point fifteen seconds behind. Oh you should've seen it."

"It isn't Usha. It is Mercy Kuttan in the 400 metre," Nari shouted.

"Mercy has got us the gold," went down the lane.

"No, no. It is Shiny Abraham in the 400 metre relay. Hip hip hurray for Shiny!"

"Yippee doo."

"Hey, the women's track events are all over anyway. Must be Vijay Amritraj who got a tennis gold."

"Yippee doo. Olympic gold!"

"Listen," I said, "I've got to tell you about our connection in Montreal."

"It's the best Carl Lewis has run, you know," Siv said. "He ran 9:93 at both Zurich and Rome but got in at 9:92 now."

"Hurray. We've won a gold," some kid was clanging a stainless steel plate with a spoon.

Siv was saying, "Our Ben actually slowed down a bit because he knew he had it all wrapped up. You should have seen the look on his face. Boy oh boy."

"Listen," I said, "Can you hear me?" because just then other voices came over crossed wires.

"Sell off the rubber shares. Just trust me and sell them. But how about the paper stocks? Hang on to those, the market is going to change ..."

While the speculators carried on their business talk, Siv went on with other statistics starting from Sudbury in 1980 when Ben was sixth with 10:88 and Lewis first with 10:43 to Seoul and 1988. The cheering human chain of neighbours and passers-by embellished their own speculations about the feats of the sixth-nine members of the Indian team.

"What about Montreal?" Siv said at one point. "Any changes in your schedule?"

"No," I said, "nothing at all. Bunto and I will be in Manipeg exactly as scheduled, Tuesday evening."

Which was just as well because the flight into Montreal was three and a half hours late and what with having to clear customs and what not, we barely made it aboard the Manipeg flight for which we had been scheduled.

Bunto, who had been awake and fidgeting all the way from London to Montreal and had thrown a royal tantrum at the customs officer and driven the stewardesses up the wall during the last lap of our trip, suddenly fell asleep as I stepped off the plane at Manipeg.

As I stood on the escalator going down to the baggage carousel and the cluster of people waiting to receive passengers, I had my first sight of Siv. He had grown a beard, or was trying to. He looked quite ghastly. I cursed Don Johnson, prophet of the unshaven look. Siv looked quite, quite ghastly, and as he ran his hand through his hair I noticed that his hair too was quite wildly ill-groomed. But still and all, breathes there a woman with soul so dead who to herself hath never said, "This is my own my much loved spouse ..."?

But something was wrong for sure. He patted Bunto's cheek and asked about the flight etc. in a tone that said he didn't really want to know.

"Is anything wrong?" I asked hesitantly.

"Oh, you haven't heard the bad news, then?"

My mouth got all dry and my stomach went into a cramp. "What news?" I asked urgently.

He calmed me with his hand. "Don't worry. I'll tell you later. You've had a long journey. I thought you'd have heard already."

With that he went off to get a cart for the suitcases.

Father, I knew it had to be Father because Mother had always had all kinds of ailments but Father was the fit one, and it is always the fit ones who go first. I felt ill and empty.

We walked to the car. The baby seat was not in its usual place. I sat in the front with Bunto cradled in my arms.

"Your parents okay?" he asked, drawing the car out of the parking spot.

So it wasn't Father or Mother, thank god. Which meant it was someone else. Who? Who? I wanted to ask but was tongue-tied.

"I've had a terrible day," he said, switching on the radio. Meech Lake, Free Trade, the newsman was droning out the usual pronouncements.

The silence between us was deafening. I pinched Bunto so we could have the distraction of his voice. But he refused to wake up.

I remembered that Siv's Uncle Sami was visiting the U.S. He had looked after Siv through his teens, when his own father had been posted in little places far from any good schools. He had built up a thriving business. A year ago he had a massive stroke that just about did him in. On returning from the hospital, he had announced he was going to live it up during the days left him and had sold his business. Last I'd heard of him was during my visit to my in-laws' when they'd got a letter from his granddaughter that he had taken every ride in Disneyland and had wanted more. Montezuma's Revenge at Knottsbury Farm had probably got him, I thought. And what did one do now? Would they fly his body back home to Madras? If we were to die tomorrow would we want our bodies flown back? Not me, I knew, but no one else knew that about me. God, god, we should talk about these things some time or another before it is too late. Poor Uncle. Poor Siv who probably loved him more than he loved his father.

On the radio, some panellists were talking about the Olympics, about the pressure that drove athletes to drugs, and the commercial greed of sponsors who were willing to pay a million dollars to whoever could set right their athlete's torn ligaments or whatever.

"Now you know," Siv said moodily.

Yes, the suspense was over, sad though it was that poor Uncle Sami was gone.

"He was a good man," I said commiseratively, placing my hand on Siv's knee.

"I am not so sure," he replied gloomily, "no matter what the pressure from others, oneself alone is responsible for one's actions."

What a harsh thing to say, I thought, there's always hoards of secret resentments in every close relationship that others don't know about.

But suddenly it struck me that maybe it wasn't Uncle Sami. O god, of course it wasn't. It was Siv's brother whose suicidal streak I thought had been set straight years ago. He now had a wonderful wife and two great kids but he had at one stage of his life tried to ... oh god, how terrible!

We reached home in silence. What a sad homecoming, I thought. Poor Siv. And now I suppose he'd have to go off to Chicago for the funeral. I felt tired, sick, empty.

Siv brought in the suitcases from the car and the newspaper from the mailbox. He flung the paper across the room. "Dammit," he shouted, "It's not just his funeral, it is ours, all of ours. Dammit, every Canadian's."

Which is when I saw the banner headlines.

The relief was so great that, hugging Bunto to my heart, I switched on all the lights in the house and then consoled wholeheartedly with my husband and my country and our poor Ben for having lost the Olympic gold.

The Icicle

The safety scanner light at the back door went on, filling the yard with light. Marzi, the neighbour's cat was the cause. She lazily rubbed herself against the caragana bush and walked away. The light shone on an icicle hanging outside the window, and diamonds flashed for a few moments through the white cloud of dryer exhaust rising from just below the window. Then the light switched itself off.

I remembered something I had forgotten to do all week — to phone Ranjit and ask if I could borrow his tripod for the weekend. I had this toy that Sivaram had given me for New Year's, a Camcorder, and I was going to take the most fantastic clips during the next few weeks — like of the diamonds glistening off the icicle. I also had to tell stories on video for my grandchildren, stories that my children had been asking me for years and that I had never got around to writing. What did it matter if the grandchildren were not born yet? One of these days they would arrive. As one of my tennis friends said, she had come to the point where she didn't care if her daughters never got married as long as they provided her with grandchildren.

Yes, I had to make video documentaries of how each of the stuffed toys we had adopted over the years had come home. Like Rakesh, the raccoon, who had been sitting rather forlornly in a corner at a garage sale down the lane until I had swept him into my arms and brought him home, given him a Lysol bath, and surgically replaced his tail.

The Camcorder was state of the art — everything Sivaram buys is state of the art, he's one of those classy men who'd never ask the price of things, or god forbid go to a garage sale. I looked forward to using it but I had just figured out that the guys on television, who slung their state-of-the-art equipment easy as easy over their shoulders, were carnivores and could probably lift twice their weight without so much as a heave. Salad-eating vegan that I am, I needed a tripod.

Maybe Ranjit had already left for Saskatoon, as he had every weekend since Deepa and little Anji had moved there. I phoned. He was still at home. "Come on over," he said, "I just came in, a little late getting back from work, not starting for Saskatoon till tomorrow, so come on over."

It took me half an hour to clear the table, stack the dirty dishes in the dishwasher, hang out the shirts from the clothes dryer etc. I got into my coat. "Hnhn," Sivaram grunted, as I said bye, bye. The six o'clock news was still on and so he probably had not registered what I'd said. That's what "hnhn" meant. "Okay!" meant my comment had been entered and his mind would process it later. "Drive carefully" meant he had really heard and registered at the same time, especially that I was taking his Volvo. Ranjit lived less than a mile away, and so the car had hardly got warm when I was at his door. Don't believe everything of what salesmen and other owners say about a Volvo. We've always had a Volvo, but that's another story.

Ranjit opened the door. "Come on in," he said, "I just have to turn off my computer."

"What are you surfing?" I asked, pretending to know all the right jargon. "Just reading a chess column," he said, "did you hear about how Kasparov got beaten by a computer?"

In one corner were stacked a couple of cartons, a child's desk and a huge stuffed toy, a panda. This one was white with black eyes the way pandas are supposed to be, unlike our Rakesh, who was blue and had white-rimmed black eyes and a black-ringed blue tail. So we'd never figured out whether he was a panda or a raccoon.

I moved some newspapers from the sofa to the table so I could sit. The couch had a couple of pillows and the recliner a blanket. Both couch and recliner were angled just right for the screen of the television set, which was on the Sports Channel. I figured, from the plates and potato chips and beer mug on the sidetables that Ranjit lived in the living room whenever he was home. Moving from recliner to couch when he wanted a change. The house had a musty winter smell, of cooking spices, cigarette smoke and beer, that had piled up in the closed rooms. In a few minutes, as always with such smells, I got used to it.

"Can I get you a cup of coffee?" he said, bringing the tripod to the living room.

"So tell me all the news," he said.

"Not a one," I said.

"Come on, Maru. Who has had a baby, who is getting married etc. etc. Or tell me about your volunteer work: how is the old cow, your boss?"

"Don't be such a gossip, Ranjit. How are you doing?"

"Till Deepa moved, I had a direct line to community happenings; now I am totally out of everything. Just me and my work, waiting for the weekend."

"You haven't missed even one weekend, eh?" I said admiringly.

"Not me, Maru. Anji will never be four again. I just can't miss out on this. It is so incredibly precious. Each week it is like she's grown. She can't wait to tell me what she has learnt at day-care. I am so glad we got her into the University day-care. She loves it. And Deepa can study without worrying, that's a great help."

"But isn't it tiring for you driving all the way Friday and Sunday evenings?"

"No sweat, just a straight road that you can drive on with eyes closed. Oh, you should see the way she throws herself onto our bed Saturday morning. We let Mom sleep in and take off. Did you know she's started adding? I took her an abacus a few weeks ago, and now you should see her! She is so much into drawing too. I am taking her this desk, see the way it opens up like a little easel, get it? Marty made it for his kids, and now it's mine. Ho-ho-ho. Being a parent is like being Santa Claus all year round. Shit, I miss not having her here."

"No denying you are Santa," I said. "The basement is so chock full of toys. You really should think of donating the playpen and stroller and carseat and what not before they get mildewed down there."

He put his hands behind his back and looked out the window.

"Would be nice to have another kid," he said. "Not good to be an only child." He turned and looked at me. "I worry, Maru, I do. Life is so unpredictable. Who knows how long we'd be around to take care of her? I mean, she needs people, family. Like, I just lift up the receiver and talk to my brother in Jaipur."

"When did you call him last?" I laughed.

"That's not the point. I know my brother and sisters are there for me, no matter where we are ... I'd like to buy a safe car, you know what I mean? I worry ... our other car is a jalopy, much worse than the one I have here ... 'It is just for within the city,' Deepa says and shrugs it off. But did you know that most accidents take place within ten kilometres of home? Every weekend I think I'll leave my car there but face it, I can't afford to take risks — a couple of weekends ago, there was this behemoth of an accident just ahead of me — not until Anji is a little older at least, and Deepa lands a job, maybe."

"Ranjit, you are turning into a worry wart. Come to think of it, you've always been one. So how's your new job?"

"No big deal. Same paper shuffling and boring programming, but at least I don't have to be on the road all the time and work up sales. Less money but this one leaves me free weekends. And that's worth everything else put together. Anji will never be four again, Maru. Oh, you've got to come with me some weekend and see for yourself."

"I'd love to see her, I said. No chance of them coming over some long weekend? It is months since they were here."

"Oh, I don't know. Deepa is always rather busy. These courses with practicals keep students hopping. She's also working with some Nursing Home where her prof. has a project going. She's doing very well, though. Straight A's all the way."

I could hear the pride in his voice. I remembered, too, his frustration three years ago when Deepa was looking for work. "It burns me up, Maru," he had said, "to see her working in Henry Armstrong's Instant Printing. For godsake, I mean, she is a straight A student and they are saying her Delhi degrees don't count, so she ends up replacing toners in bloody photocopy machines. Sometimes I think I should run for the Legislature and get some action going, really. Pisses me off, all this racism. Say, did I show you her grad pics from last fall? I took them with this tripod and my Canon."

"Yes, Ranj, you did, about a dozen times if you want to know, though I'd be delighted to look at them, all fifty of them, over again if you could find the album under all this rubble."

He moved his hands in a one-two punch at me. "Aye, Maru," he said, "you're a one."

I took out the pop-up picture book I had brought for Anji. "From what you say," I said, "maybe she's outgrown this already."

He smiled proudly. "She's my daughter, never forget that, Maru. Say, have I told you how her name is just so right, though I never realized it when I insisted on naming her that?"

"Anjali? an offering, as in Tagore's 'Gitanjali'?" I remembered him reciting Tagore soon after her birth.

"Yeah, that too. But I mean Anji as in inside Ranjit. Got it?" He placed his hand on his heart. "Shit. Why is it only women get to carry the tykes inside?"

"I'd better be going," I said, "It has started snowing already. They are forecasting heavy snow for tomorrow."

"Oh, shit. Really? He took up the remote control and switched to The Weather Channel. "Oh, shit. I thought of leaving early morning. I guess I'd better get started rightaway and beat the blizzard. Oh, shit. Sorry to boot you out, Maru. Thanks for dropping by."

"I should be thanking you," I said.

"Any time, Maru, any time. You can keep the tripod till the cows come home. All my gear is out in Saskatoon, and by now I've got it all figured out how to sit my Camcorder on my shoulder."

"You have? Tell me the secret."

He smiled. "Uh unh. Okay, seeing as you are my best friend and all, you can get it at any photo place — Don's, Astral, Japan Camera ..."

He put on his coat and took up his overnight satchel. He picked up the panda from the sofa. "I guess the other things will have to wait till next Friday. So what do you think your name is going to be?" he said, giving the panda a squeeze.

"Panduranga," I said, "Tell Anji his name is Panduranga the panda. But wait, what do I ask for? A shoulder strap?"

"I love your ignorance, Maru, love you." He smiled. He had a charming smile, a little boy's smile, his eyes dancing with light. It made my heart ache to see that smile, and my eyes wandered to the bookshelf where, within a diamond-studded glass frame, he and Anji flanked Deepa in her baccalaureate convocation gown. I went up to him and gave him a hug. "Drive carefully, little brother," I said, using the diminutive of my own Tamil language which could better express the gut-wrenching affection and sadness I felt for him. "Drive carefully, little brother, and give my love to Deepa and Anji."

We walked out of the house together, he to his battered Toyota, I to Sivaram's new Volvo. Can't he see? I cried to myself, the whole convocation album scrolling on my mental screen, he so happy and proud and hugging her in every photograph of them, and she drawing away from his touch. It was only a matter of time.

*****

"First name in fashion designs, sixth letter 'i'," Sivaram said, his pencil poised over the morning crossword. "And Michael Jackson's famous gait. Take a break, who can remember such old hat?"

"Moonwalk," I said. "You always get the answer to clues like Scarlett's locale or one of the Musketeers."

"Those are classics. There's a difference, in case you haven't thought about it. I can wager even kids now fifteen wouldn't know Michael Jackson from a hole in the wall. By the way, I have to go to Saskatoon first weekend of next month."

"Great," I said. "I'll come along."

He lowered his head and looked at me from above his reading glasses. "Saskatoon, not Sweden or Sasquatch. You want to come to Saskatoon? As in Regina-Saskatoon?"

"Yes, sure do. Meet some old friends. Like Deepa. She called me just yesterday, and today you tell me you have a meeting in Saskatoon. Don't you think there's something to the coincidence?"

"Like divine providence leading you?"

I shrugged, "Why not?" There was no need to tell him that Deepa called me routinely once every few weeks.

"Is she still out there? Maybe that explains it. I ran into Ranjit the other day and he looked out of sorts. Or maybe he's lost some hair or weight or something. He looked different. Are they still together?"

"Of course they are together."

"Okay, okay, don't blow a fuse. Your feminist crowd break-up all the time, even lesbians, I mean. So what is Deepa doing? Physiotherapy, isn't it?"

"She is working on her Master's," I said. "Doing very well, too. She hopes to get an assistantship soon."

"You mean you're going to let her join the slave-pack?" He smiled. That had been one of our frequent points of dissension. In recent years, he had taken to bringing over graduate students from India, and paying them peanuts. I felt he was exploiting them. He maintained that he was doing them a favour. We had this argument every little while.

Did I know of the recent changes in Immigration policy? That if one wasn't related to someone already here or wasn't an entrepreneur with a million dollars, there was absolutely no way one could get into the country? Six percent was all they admitted in the Independent category, did I know that? "In our days, if we had brains, we could come help both ourselves and the country get ahead. I mean what future was there for Canada if we only allowed six percent as independents? So our people," he still said 'our people' even though he had spent more of his life outside India than in, "can come in only as students. Not with a job or even as post-Docs, as most of us did. No, not even for a PhD because, of course, no one had grants to support them. Only as grad students in the Master's program," so he chooses these bright young men from middle class families and gives them a foothold into the country.

"And peanuts," I said.

"So what if they lived for a year or two in basement rooms along Silverstone and Townsend, and on peanuts and snow? Take my word, Canada will be the richer for them, which is more than I can say of my Canadian-born undergraduates, even those with parents born elsewhere."

"If they don't run off to the States," I said.

"If Immigration would admit more graduate students instead of reintegrating so-called families and having to monitor and/or encourage marriages of convenience by opportunists ..."

The argument always ended in a tie.

"Ranjit is supporting her all the way, of course, but an assistantship would help," I said, remembering what Ranjit had told me about wanting a safe car.

"Would you please phone me around eleven today so I can get Beth to book your ticket along with mine? And whether you'll be staying with me or with Deepa. Unless, of course, you think I shouldn't ask Beth."

That was another of our bones of contention — the way bosses asked their secretaries to make the coffee and do their personal work.

"I'll stay with you Thursday, for sure," I said. "The first evening is always fun at your conferences. Giorgio," I said, "Giorgio Armani. And isn't Sasquatch a yeti or something?"

"Thanks," he said, "Didn't think you'd notice. Just assume I said Surabaya or Swaziland," and went on to solve the day's cryptogram.

*****

Deepa came to our hotel at nine that Friday morning to pick me up. The first thing that hit me was that she was looking beautiful. A kind of glow that can come only from within. I hadn't seen her like that since the time Anji was about due.

While Ranjit hovered and worried himself sick over her, she just sat smiling, with that glow on and around her, as though she knew everything about her birthing would be, could not but be, perfectly normal.

How happy they had been then, those last few months and the first few months. Ranj did everything around the house, cooked and cleaned, and washed the dirty diapers — no rash-prone non-eco-conscious disposables or diaper service for his baby, nothing but cotton diapers laundered at home and aired in the sun. Did I know the Vitamin A in the sun was good even for clothes?

"It's going to work out so well," Deepa said, "that you've come on a Friday. I am taking the day off and Anji will be at day-care till four and that will leave us the time to catch up on all the news."

"You are looking gorgeous," I said, getting into her car. "Looks like you like what you are doing.

"Oh, yes, yes, yes," she said, "every minute of it."

She told me about her work, her classes, her professor's project. Massage therapy, meditation, holistic care. He was trying to tabulate and formulate why the body reacted the way it did, and please don't tell me people in India and China knew all about it centuries ago. She was more interested in the actual results. To see a wasted limb get back to being functional ... it was so tangible, so real, so worthwhile.

I was being carried onto her high.

We went to her department, where she had a few chores to finish. I sat in her cubicle and flipped through some journals while she did her work. The cubicle was piled high with library books: on the table, the shelves, the floor. Only the computer desk in the corner was neat and functional. Beside it was stacked the first draft of the first chapter of her thesis.

It was creditable how far she had come and how fast. It was less than a year since she had started her Master's program. I felt proud of her, my protege.

The years of her Bachelor's program had been rough, not because of her skills or time, but because she knew the crossroads that awaited her once she had her degree. She had delayed completing her program, while she endlessly debated with herself as to what she should do. I was the only one privy to her debates. She would talk and talk Just my being there so she could debate aloud helped her get the courage to take her decision. She knew very well what she wanted to do but she needed the time to process it through her psychological channels, to arrive at a point when she could live with herself for taking the decision.

Now I sat back and listened to the sound of her voice as she discussed something with a colleague in another cubicle. Technical jargon flowed back and forth, and there was so much confidence in her tone as she debated the issue. I didn't listen to what was being said, but I was filled with delight at how happy she sounded, and when she laughed, it was so carefree, like she was home free.

We went to her apartment. It was just four blocks from the university, and overlooked a playground. "I have been so lucky all the way," Deepa said, "Anji just loves to stand on the sofa and watch the playground while I get dinner ready. Not that I cook much. Anji has a good breakfast; she is addicted to her cheese sandwich for lunch; milk and an apple when she comes home. But dinner has to be coaxed in, spoon by spoon. Thank god she eats vegetables and all that at least during the weekends."

"So when are you coming to Manipeg?" I said at some point. "You used to come often enough but you haven't been there for, how long?"

"I am not counting," she said, "The longer the better. Those weekends used to wipe me out. I ended up cooking and cleaning all day every day, feeding all the people who had invited him over in my absence; I had to slog to pay for what he had enjoyed. Ugh. And the house was always such a mess. Knowing I would come, he never lifted a finger between my visits. Not that he helped in any way when I was there, for that matter. He has been a couch potato ever since I went back to university. I had to earn my tuition fees, that is the way he saw it, I guess. Wonder what he does now. Gets a cleaning woman, I suppose."

I was not ready to answer. But she did not seem to expect or want an answer. She went on to talk about Anji.

"She must love having him here every weekend," I said.

"Why wouldn't she," she said, "He spoils her rotten."

"Children can be spoilt but there's no such thing as being spoilt rotten," I said. "Love is one commodity that never stales."

"I can handle love," she said. "Anything that doesn't occupy space or can be eaten up. But he brings her things every weekend. Just look around you, Maru," she said. "Soon we won't have any room to move. See that desk? He brought it a few weeks ago, it is supposed to be an easel for his daughter's masterpieces. Really. And the stuffed toys! You won't believe the size of the panda he brought the time we had that storm — I don't know if you had it out there. And father and kid give names to each of these stuffed animals. It takes Anji half an hour every day to say goodnight to her toys. Really, he spoils her rotten. It takes me two days to get her back on track. And two days later he's here again. UND has a better program, you know, but I figured Grand Forks, and even Fargo were too close; that the eight hour drive to Saskatoon would faze him; so I chose this place. Boy, was I wrong! I sure am looking forward to the day when I can go farther than his driving distance and have Anji all to myself."

"But he loves her," I said. "It would break his heart."

"Oh," she said, "how I wish he'd just find some other woman and get out of my hair."

A Selection of Our Titles in Print

A Lad from Brantford (David Adams Richards) essays	0-921411-25-1	11.95
All the Other Phil Thompsons Are Dead (Phil Thompson) poetry	1-896647-05-7	12.95
Avoidance Tactics (Sky Gilbert) drama	1-896647-50-2	15.88
CHSR Poetry Slam (Andrew Titus, ed.) poetry	1-896647-06-5	10.95
Combustible Light (Matt Santateresa) poetry	0-921411-97-9	12.95
Cover Makes a Set (Joe Blades) poetry	0-919957-60-9	8.95
Crossroads Cant (Mary Elizabeth Grace, Mark Seabrook, Shafiq, Ann Shin. Joe Blades, ed.) poetry	0-921411-48-0	13.95
Dark Seasons (Georg Trakl; Robin Skelton, trans.) poetry	0-921411-22-7	10.95
Elemental Mind (K.V. Skene) poetry	1-896647-16-2	10.95
for a cappuccino on Bloor (kath macLean) poetry	0-921411-74-X	13.95
Gift of Screws (Robin Hannah) poetry	0-921411-56-1	12.95
Heaven of Small Moments (Allan Cooper) poetry	0-921411-79-0	12.95
Herbarium of Souls (Vladimir Tasic) short fiction	0-921411-72-3	14.95
I Hope It Don't Rain Tonight (Phillip Igloliorti) poetry	0-921411-57-X	11.95
JC & Me (Ted Mouradian) religion	1-896647-35-9	15.99
Jive Talk: George Fetherling in Interviews and Documents George Fetherling (Joe Blades, ed.)	1-896647-54-5	13.95
Like Minds (Shannon Friesen) short fiction	0-921411-81-2	14.95
Manitoba highway map (rob mclennan) poetry	0-921411-89-8	13.95
Memories of Sandy Point, St. George's Bay, Newfoundland (Phyllis Pieroway) memoir, history	0-921411-33-2	14.95
New Power (Christine Lowther) poetry	0-921411-94-4	11.95
Notes on drowning (rob mclennan) poetry	0-921411-75-8	13.95
Open 24 Hours (Anne Burke, D.C. Reid, Brenda Niskala Joe Blades, rob mclennan) poetry	0-921411-64-2	13.95
Railway Station (karl wendt) poetry	0-921411-82-0	11.95
Reader be Thou Also Ready (Robert James) novel	1-896647-26-X	18.69
Rum River (Raymond Fraser) short fiction	0-921411-61-8	16.95
Seeing the World with One Eye (Edward Gates) poetry	0-921411-69-3	12.95
Shadowy:Technicians: New Ottawa Poets (rob mclennan, ed.) poetry	0-921411-71-5	16.95
Song of the Vulgar Starling (Eric Miller) poetry	0-921411-93-6	14.95
Speaking Through Jagged Rock (Connie Fife) poetry	0-921411-99-5	12.95
Starting from Promise (Lorne Dufour) poetry	1-896647-52-9	13.95
Tales for an Urban Sky (Alice Major) poetry	1-896647-11-1	13.95
The Longest Winter (Julie Doiron, Ian Roy) photos, fiction	0-921411-95-2	18.69
The Sweet Smell of Mother's Milk-Wet Bodice (Uma Parameswaran) novella	1-896647-72-3	13.95
Túnel de proa verde / Tunnel of the Green Prow (Nela Rio; Hugh Hazelton, translator) poetry	0-921411-80-4	13.95
Wharves and Breakwaters of Yarmouth County, Nova Scotia (Sarah Petite) art, travel	1-896647-13-8	17.95
What Morning Illuminates (Suzanne Hancock) poetry	1-896647-18-9	4.95
What Was Always Hers (Uma Parameswaran) fiction	1-896647-12-X	17.95

www.brokenjaw.com hosts our current catalogue, submissions guidelines, maunscript award competitions, booktrade sales representation and distribution information. Broken Jaw Press eBook of selected titles are available from http://www.PublishingOnline.Com. Directly from us, all individual orders must be prepaid. All Canadian orders must add 7% GST/HST (Canada Customs and Revenue Agency Number: 12489 7943 RT0001).
BROKEN JAW PRESS, Box 596 Stn A, Fredericton NB E3B 5A6, Canada